F
MAR   Martin, Ann M.

           Just a summer ro-
           mance

PRESENTED BY

WILTON PTA

Just a
Summer Romance

Just a
Summer Romance

ANN M. MARTIN

HOLIDAY HOUSE/NEW YORK

Library of Congress Cataloging-in-Publication Data

Martin, Ann M.,
Just a summer romance.

SUMMARY: Fourteen-year-old Melanie can't forget
the handsome, mysterious boy who was her "summer
romance," and when she sees his face on the cover of
"People" magazine, she is determined to learn the
truth about him.
I. Title.
PZ7.M3567585Ju   1987   [Fic]   86-46201
ISBN 0-8234-0649-0

This book is for my editor,
MARGERY CUYLER,
with gratitude, affection,
and thanks for her help, her foresight,
and her understanding.

PART I
Fire Island

Chapter One

Melanie Braderman settled herself comfortably in an armchair at her family's beach house. She propped her legs up on the coffee table and sighed happily. "I love the rain," she said, looking at the streaming windows.

"You're weird, you know that?" said Timmy disgustedly.

"You tell me so several times a day," replied Mel.

"And it never seems to do any good."

"Maybe it's because you're the one who's weird." Mel opened an Agatha Christie mystery and got prepared for a long, leisurely read.

"Mom!" yelled Timmy. "Mel said I was weird."

"I did not, Mom!" shouted Mel, putting her book down long enough to stick her tongue out at her brother. "But you *are* a pest. You're the Grand Pest of the World, Ruler and Leader of Pestilence, Head of—"

"Melanie! Timothy!" Mrs. Braderman stuck her head out of the kitchen. "One more cross word and you can both spend the rest of the day in your rooms. You're giving me a headache. It's too muggy to argue."

"Yeah," said Mel. "This argument's forfeited on account of mugginess."

Mrs. Braderman smiled and came into the living room. Timmy shut up. He wandered over to the screen door and stared outside at the rain.

"How long is this supposed to go on?" he asked crossly.

"No one knows," replied Mel, not looking up from her book.

"Mom?" asked Timmy again.

"Honey, I don't know," said his mother. "Where are the Reeders? Where's Jackie?"

Timmy shrugged.

"Well, why don't you go next door and find out?" she suggested. "You too, Mel."

"Are you trying to get rid of us?" asked Melanie. "I'm very happy right here. Miss Marple is on the verge of cracking this whole case wide open. And the police don't have a clue as to what's going on. . . . Get it? A *clue?*"

"When I was your age," replied Mrs. Braderman, "I was still reading Nancy Drew."

"Times are changing, Mom."

"I guess so." Mrs. Braderman sat down on the couch, curling her legs underneath her. She picked up a large needlepoint canvas and began stitching carefully.

Timmy slipped into his yellow slicker. "Okay," he announced. "I'm going to look for Jackie. If I can't find him, I'm going to the Harbor Store."

"All right, sweetie."

"Bring back some Peanut M&M's," called Melanie.

"Mel, your teeth, your complexion."

"I know, Mom," said Mel. "Mint condition. And all thanks to chocolate."

Timmy left, allowing the screen door to bang shut. Melanie could hear his bare feet slap along the wet boardwalk that led to Sea Gull Walk, which ran in front of their house.

"Mom?" asked Mel. "Do you get bored out here? Or lonely?"

"Oh, I suppose I do sometimes, sweetie. But I wouldn't want to give up the island."

"I know what you mean."

The Bradermans had been spending summers in their little beach house on Fire Island since before Melanie was born. Summer was spelled *B-E-A-C-H* as far as Melanie was concerned. She loved Fire Island, she loved the sun and sand and ocean, and she loved their cottage. It was just right for her family. There were three small bedrooms, one for her parents, one for Timmy, and one for Melanie and her older sister, Dorothy (who preferred to be called Dee). There was the living room with its wood-burning stove and the many windows that faced the bay. On hot days, the living room was breezy and cool. On cold days, it could be heated cozily by the stove.

And there was the kitchen. That was all there was to Moonrise House, and Melanie thought every square inch of it was perfect.

She even liked the name. All the houses in Davis Park had names. Some were corny. For instance, the name of the doctor's cottage was Bedside Manor. Every time Melanie showed it to someone new, she felt as if she had to say, "Get it? Bedside *Manor?*"

The only thing Mel did not like about Fire Island was that it was too far from New York City for her father to commute to work. He had to stay at their home in Bronxville by himself during the week and could only join the rest of the Bradermans on the weekends. During the summers he usually took three-day weekends, but even so, Mel thought her parents were a little lonely from Monday to Thursday when they were apart.

Mel herself almost never felt lonely. First of all, she enjoyed being alone, and second, Lacey Reeder, her summertime best friend, lived in Starfish House, the cottage next door. Lacey had just turned fourteen, which was exactly Melanie's age. Her nine-year-old brother, Jackie, was Timmy's age (and *his* summertime best friend), and their sixteen-year-old sister, Jeanmarie, was Dee's age (and *her* summertime best friend). It was a perfect arrangement, Mel thought, except for the fact that the Reeders' home was in New York City, which was why she and Lacey were only summertime best friends. They saw each other day in and day out from the end of school until Labor Day, and then only two or three times until the following summer.

Mel sighed. It was already the first week in August. Summer was on its last legs. In a little over a month she'd be back in school. Not only that, she'd be starting as a freshman at Bronxville High. She sighed again. She hated being a new kid anywhere.

"Something wrong?" asked Mrs. Braderman, looking up from her needlework.

Melanie put down her book, which she hadn't been reading at all. "I was just thinking about school."

"Mel, you've got weeks before it starts."

"Only four. At the beginning of the summer there were thirteen. I like having a big cushion between me and school."

"I thought you liked school."

"I do . . . I guess."

"Are you nervous about the high school?"

"A little. But it's worse than that. Mom, do you know that I am fourteen years old and I've never had a boy-friend? I don't think I've ever even been whistled at."

"Count your blessings. But I don't see any good reason *why* you've never been whistled at."

Mel stretched out her legs and looked at them. They were nice and tan after nine weeks in the sun, but Mel frowned. "My legs are too skinny. *I'm* too skinny."

"You've got lovely brown eyes and beautiful hair. Most people would give their eyeteeth for hair like yours."

It was true. Mel did have nice hair. It was a rich, dark brown that streaked red in the sun. And it had just enough wave so that Mrs. Braderman assured Melanie she'd never have to spend a hundred dollars to get it permed.

"Well, where are my lovely eyes and beautiful hair getting me?" asked Mel. "Dee's had thousands of boy-friends. Some of them could go right up on a Hunk-of-the-Month calendar."

"Dee's older."

"Dee's prettier."

"Hello!" called a voice from the front door.

"Come in, Lacey," said Mrs. Braderman, "and do something about Melanie. She's wallowing in self-pity."

Lacey grinned and hung up her raincoat by the screen door.

Mel studied Lacey critically as she crossed the room and sat down next to Mrs. Braderman on the couch. If Mel was pretty, then Lacey was gorgeous. And of course, being from New York City, she was sophisticated. Very sophisticated. Her hair really was permed. Furthermore, it was blond. At least, it had started the summer that way. By August, thanks to the sun, it was blonder than blond. It was the color of cornsilk. And Lacey was tall, tan, not too thin, always wore designer clothes, and had never, ever had a pimple. Anywhere. Sometimes Mel felt plain and ordinary next to Lacey. But she knew that Lacey, who tended to be shy, valued Mel's imagination and sense of humor. In the end, Mel thought, they balanced each other nicely.

"Well, I know something that will make Mel feel better," said Lacey.

"What?" asked Mel.

"I just heard the weather report. Clearing tonight. Sunny and hot tomorrow."

"Goody," said Mel. "But you know I don't mind the rain."

"I know. But rain is fine, beach is better, I always say." Mel giggled. "You do?"

"Always," replied Lacey. "Want to play Trivia Chase?"

"Sure. Want to play, Mom?"

"Why not?" replied Mrs. Braderman.

"Let's pig out while we're at it," added Mel, jumping up and making a dash for the kitchen.

"Mel, your teeth, your complexion."

"You worry too much, Mom."

"I can't help it. I'm your mother. Mothers worry."

"Well, worry about getting me a boyfriend. That's a more pressing problem."

Mel returned to the living room with a bag of potato chips, a quart of ice cream, and a package of brownies. "Okay, let's play."

Lacey had been right. The weather cleared, and the next morning Mel woke to the sounds of sea gulls crying and birds rustling the shrubbery outside her bedroom window. That was another thing she liked about Davis Park. It wasn't barren and open like most beach areas. It was lush and green. Trees and shrubs grew everywhere. When she was in the center of the island, Mel could almost imagine that she was lost in a large forest—except for the sound of waves breaking not far away. And she really did feel far from civilization. Davis Park had a restaurant on the beach, a tiny post office, fire-station, police station, and a general store and ice-cream stand by the docks on the bay side, but that was it. No shops, no movie theaters. Cars weren't even allowed on that part of the island. There were no roads for them. People pulled red wagons along the boardwalks instead.

Mel stretched luxuriously and pushed aside the window shade to get a look outside. She saw a sparkling blue sky and bright sunshine.

Across the room, Dee moaned and rolled over. "Put the shade back," she mumbled.

"But Dee, it's a beautiful day. Come on, get up. Let's go to the beach right now. We can spend the whole day there."

"In a minute."

Mel knew that Dee's "in a minute" could mean anywhere from thirty seconds to several hours. She changed into her bathing suit and tiptoed into the living room, where she discovered that she was the only one up. She didn't care. She liked having the early morning hours to herself. Mel made a cup of tea and took it out to the front deck. She was about to sit down with it when Lacey wandered onto her deck next door. Mel waved. Lacey waved back and ran down Starfish's walk and up Moonrise's.

"Hi," she whispered.

"Hi. Let's eat breakfast on the beach and spend the whole day there."

"Good idea."

Mel drank her tea quickly, and she and Lacey gathered their things together and set out for the beach.

Mel enjoyed early morning on the beach. It wasn't deserted—she saw several joggers, two people walking their dogs, a woman with a baby on her back, and two men and a woman fishing—but it was quieter than at any other time of the day.

She and Lacey spread out their towels and dug into a breakfast of doughnuts and orange juice. Two hours later Timmy and Mrs. Braderman joined them. A half an hour later the rest of the Reeders showed up, and an hour after *that*, Dee struggled down to the beach.

"Let's play Frisbee," Timmy suggested.

"Okay," agreed Mel. "Come on, Lace."

Mel, Lacey, Timmy, and Jackie ran to the water's edge.

Timmy let the Frisbee fly, and—*crack!*—it struck a boy full in the face.

Mel gasped. "Timmy, you klutz!"

She ran to the boy, who was holding his hands over his nose. "Are you all right?" she asked him. "I'm really sorry. My brother didn't mean to hit you. Sometimes he doesn't aim too well."

Timmy kicked Mel's ankle and she made a face at him.

The boy, who was about Mel's age, took his hands from his nose and blinked at Mel, Timmy, Lacey, and Jackie, who had crowded around him. "I think I'll live," he said pleasantly. "It wasn't traveling very fast."

"Are you sure?" asked Mel. "We could walk you over to Bedside Manor."

"Bedside Manor?"

"You know, the doctor's."

"Oh, no. I'm fine. Really."

Mel looked at the boy's face. It seemed all right—no
bump or bruise. In fact, it seemed better than all right.
Mel suddenly decided it was the most gorgeous face she'd
ever seen. Wide-set brown eyes looked back at her from
under a mop of dark curls. A handful of freckles were
scattered across his nose. And a grin that lit up his entire
face.

"Well, I better be going," said the boy. "See you." He
smiled, waved, and began walking away.

"Wait!" cried Mel.

The boy turned around. "What?"

"It's . . . nothing. See you," replied Mel.

The boy waved again and walked on.

Timmy and Jackie ran into the ocean, the Frisbee forgotten.

Mel turned to Lacey. "I think I'm in love," she said.

Chapter Two

Mel and Lacey stayed on the beach until long after what Mel thought of as "prime time." By five o'clock, when the sun was growing weaker and people were starting to gather their sandy possessions and head for their houses, Lacey stood up. "Mel, I've got to go," she said. "I need a shower. I smell like seaweed. Mom and everyone left half an hour ago."

Mel barely heard her. She was scanning the beach for the gorgeous boy Timmy had smashed with the Frisbee. She'd been watching hopefully for him all day.

"Mel?" said Lacey.

"What?"

"Earth to Mel. Earth to Mel. Come in, Mel. Over."

Mel giggled. "Sorry. What did you say?"

Lacey sighed. "I feel like a broken record. Ever since

13

you saw that boy, I've had to repeat everything I say to
you. I said I'm going back to the house now. It's late.
Aren't you coming?"

"I guess." Mel rose reluctantly and shook out her towel.
She threw her Agatha Christie book and her tape player
into her beach bag and ambled toward Moonrise, dragging
along behind Lacey.

"He probably hasn't spent much time on Fire Island,"
Mel commented as they passed Bedside Manor.

"What?" said Lacey. "Who hasn't?"

"That boy. Everyone in Davis Park knows what Bedside Manor is."

"Well, maybe he just hasn't been to Davis Park before."

"Nope," said Mel. "He hasn't been on the beach this
summer. Did you notice his skin? It hasn't seen the light
of day in weeks."

"Detective Mel," said Lacey. "I think you've been reading too many mysteries."

Mel smiled. "Well, it pays off. I mean, already I know
two things about him. One, he's new here, and two, he's
just beginning his vacation."

"What do you mean, 'already'?"

"Hmm," replied Mel. "I'm not sure."

Lacey looked at Mel over her shoulder. "You're acting
weird."

"You know, Timmy said the same thing to me just
yesterday."

"You're hopeless."

"Hopeless, too? Weird and hopeless. That doesn't sound
very promising."

Lacey giggled. "Want to get ice cream after dinner?"

"Are you kidding? A scoop of cookies 'n' cream contains sugar, fat, and, most important, chocolate. All the right ingredients. Of course I want to get ice cream."

"Good. Come over after dinner."

"Okay. See you."

"See you." The girls separated at the walk to Moonrise House.

Mel waited until almost nine o'clock before going next door to the Reeders'. There was something exciting and also uniquely summery about getting ice-cream cones after dark. Mel liked the feel of walking through the blackness, the night air warm and breezy, and emerging from the trees onto the dimly lit boat docks.

At the Reeders', Mel and Lacey each tucked a dollar bill into their pocket before they set out for the ice-cream stand. The docks were busy as usual. The people who owned boats and were spending several days at Davis Park were lounging around on their decks, barbecuing hamburgers or visiting with friends. The island people streamed in and out of the little store, and a long line of people were waiting for cones at the stand next door.

Mel and Lacey joined the end of the line.

"I guess you'll get cookies 'n' cream as usual," Lacey said to Mel. "Let's see. Tonight it'll be a toss-up for me. Either butterscotch or chocolate-chip. Or maybe chocolate-chip mint. Or maybe just plain vanilla. If you weren't getting cookies 'n' cream, what would you get instead? Mel? . . . *Mel?*"

Mel wasn't listening. She was staring at the head of the line. Lacey followed her gaze. "What is it?" she asked, peering into the darkness.

"It's *him,*" Mel whispered. "The boy on the beach."

Lacey rolled her eyes. "So what?"

"I want to see what flavor he's getting. And I want to see who he's with." Mel craned her neck around. "It looks like . . . yeah, I think he's getting fudge ripple. Now he's paying the guy . . . now he's getting his change. . . . He's putting it in his pocket. . . . He's licking a drip on the side of his cone. . . . Hey, he's all alone! He's not with anybody! He's just walking toward the Harbor Store. Gosh, that's sad. All alone in a great place like Fire Island. I wonder what he has to buy at the store."

"Mel, do you know what? You are crazy. You are loony tunes."

"I've got bats in my belfry."

"Rats in your attic."

"I'm a few bricks short of a load."

"A few cards short of a deck."

"The shingles are loose on my roof."

"You're balmy."

"I am not of sound mind."

"What'll it be, girls?"

Mel looked up, startled. She'd had no idea the line was moving so quickly. "You go first," she said to Lacey.

"I'll have, um . . . I'll have a scoop of butterscotch. In a cone, please."

The boy behind the counter handed Lacey a cone.

"And I'll have a scoop of fudge ripple in a cone, please,"

said Mel. She glanced sideways to find Lacey staring at her. "Well, it looked good," she said defensively. "And it still has all the right ingredients—sugar, fat, and chocolate."

Lacey just shook her head. "All right," she said at last. "Let's go to the store."

"The store? I don't need anything."

"I thought you'd want to see what *he* was doing. Maybe find out what brand of dental floss *he* uses."

"Oh, *he's* already gone. I've been watching. I guess *he* didn't buy anything. *He* walked right back out just as you were telling me I'm a few cards short of a deck."

Lacey giggled. "You are certifiably insane. Let's go."

The next day, Mel saw the boy two more times. The first time was early in the morning. Mrs. Braderman had sent Mel to the Harbor Store to buy the *New York Times*. When Mel came out, carrying the paper gingerly so as not to get newsprint on her bathing suit, she noticed that the ferry had arrived from Patchogue. She paused to see who was coming over to the island so early on a weekday morning. That was when she saw *him*. He was waiting patiently at the end of the dock. Presently a middle-aged man with curly gray hair stepped off the ferry. He saw the boy immediately and held his arms wide open for a hug.

The second time she saw *him* was late in the afternoon. The tide was out, and he was clamming on the bay side of the island. "All alone again," Mel remarked to Lacey that evening.

The next day, Thursday, Mel spotted *him* leaving the Harbor Store. "Still alone. I think it's so sad. And beautiful."

Lacey raised her eyebrows. "Beautiful?"

"He must be very lonely, but he always seems so . . . serene. That's it. He seems serene. Like he's at peace with himself."

"Mel, he's not *dy*ing."

"Well, you know what I mean. But he's kind of mysterious, too. And I'll tell you something. Before we leave the island this summer, I am going to get to know him. I, Melanie Braderman, will crack that shell he's hiding in and get to know the beautiful, secretive soul inside."

"Bonkers," was all Lacey would say. "Stark, raving mad."

Chapter Three

On Saturday morning, Mel and Lacey woke up early enough to see the sunrise. Mel slapped her alarm off the second it began to ring, and leaped out of bed. She had slept in her bathing suit, so it took her only a few moments to get ready. She grabbed her sweat shirt and slipped it on as she ran barefoot through the chilly gray dawn to the Reeders' house.

Mel scratched softly on the screened window to the bedroom that Lacey and Jeanmarie shared. "Hey," she whispered. "Lacey! . . . Lacey!"

Lacey's sleepy face appeared. "I'll be right there," she mumbled.

"Okay, but hurry. We always manage to miss this."

Lacey had slept in her bathing suit, too. In exactly three minutes, she stepped onto her front deck, also barefoot, also wearing a sweat shirt. A camera dangled by its strap from her wrist.

"You're going to photograph the sunrise?" Mel asked. "I don't think anything will come out."

"Well, I'm going to try. I've seen other pictures of sunrises, so I know it can be done."

"Come on," said Mel. "Let's go."

The girls ran quietly down the walk and along a network of wooden boardwalks.

The last walk ended above the ocean at the top of the dunes. The girls found themselves looking down on the crashing ocean, gray in the early light, and a misty, deserted beach.

"We made it!" Mel exclaimed in a whisper. "Look! It's just beginning."

On the horizon, the tip of a brilliant orangey-pink disk had appeared, staining the ocean with wavery bands of color.

"Shall we watch from up here or go down to the sand?" asked Mel.

"Let's stay here," replied Lacey, hugging her sweat shirt about her. "This is a great view. And I bet the sand is cold."

The girls settled down at the top of the wooden stairs that led to the beach. Lacey clicked her camera every few seconds, as the sun climbed the sky.

Mel was enchanted. She couldn't take her eyes from the sight.

But when Lacey exclaimed, "Hey, I'm out of film," she shook herself back to reality.

That was when she noticed that they were not alone. Somebody else had enjoyed the spectacle. A figure in a green windbreaker was huddled, knees drawn to his chest, in the sand a little distance down the beach.

It was the boy.

As Mel watched him, he rose slowly, brushed the sand from his long legs, and began striding down the beach toward the western end of the island.

"That's him!" Mel whispered loudly. "There he is! Come on, I'm going to follow him! Maybe we can find out where he lives."

"You can't do that!" exclaimed Lacey. "It's invasion of privacy."

"Oh, he'll never know. We'll keep a safe distance. Hurry! He's a fast walker." Mel was already halfway down the stairs. "If he turns around and sees us, he'll just think we're out for an early walk. This is a public beach. We're allowed. Look, there's a guy walking his dog. We're not the only people on the beach anymore."

Mel was jogging along, trying to keep up with the boy. Lacey ran beside her. "I don't know, Mel. I think you've gone nuts."

Mel didn't answer. She concentrated on pumping her legs up and down.

She and Lacey followed the boy for five minutes. "Where is he *going*?" Mel asked finally. "We're almost out of Davis Park."

"Maybe he's taking a twenty-mile hike," said Lacey. "I hope your legs are prepared for it. Mine aren't. In exactly two more minutes, I am turning back."

But before two minutes were up, the boy suddenly veered to his right and cut across the sand toward a flight of wooden steps.

Mel looked around. They were on an isolated stretch of beach. The area in which she and Lacey lived was crowded, the homes close-set, even those nearest the water. From where she stood then, however, Mel could see only one house, a rambling, older home with oddly placed sun decks and terraces.

Mel waited until the boy had climbed the flight of steps. Then she hurried across the sand after him. Lacey followed, shaking her head. At the top of the steps, Mel paused and looked down the boardwalk. It was deserted. She ran along it until it intersected with the walk to a house. Mel peered up the walk. And there was the boy, rinsing his sandy feet with the hose before going inside his house.

Mel pulled back, putting a row of shrubbery between herself and the boy. "It's the house we saw from the beach," she whispered to Lacey.

"Amazing," replied Lacey. "Now let's go home. I'm starved. I want breakfast."

"Go *home?*" Mel exclaimed. "But we just got here. This is the closest I've come to finding out anything about—"

"About *him?*"

"Yes. About *him.* Come on. I want to go back to the beach. The view of his house is much better from there."

"You mean we're going to *spy* on him? Mel, I can't

do that. I don't want to do that. You know what? You're obsessed."

"I am not."

"Are too."

"All right, I'm obsessed. I still want to go back to the dunes and watch for a while. Maybe he'll sit out on one of his decks. Maybe he'll eat his breakfast there. I wonder if I'll be able to tell what he's eating."

Mel turned and trotted back along the boardwalk. She ran down to the beach, scouted around in the sand dunes, sat down, and looked at the house. Then she stood up, moved over slightly, and sat down again.

"What are you doing?" asked Lacey as Mel stood up once again.

"Trying to get the best view of his house, somewhere where I can see but not be seen. The trouble is, I don't *know* whether I can be seen. Oh, well." Mel sat down and patted the sand beside her. "Sit, Lace. It's actually pretty comfortable here. You can lean back against this dune."

"Mel, I am not sitting down. I am going home to have breakfast. Then I am going to spend the day reading on the beach like a normal American."

"Not all Americans spend their days reading on beaches."

"And statistics show that even fewer spend them lolling around in sand dunes, spying on boys their brothers hit with Frisbees."

"Well, anyway, do me a favor. After you eat breakfast,

could you bring me Jackie's binoculars? I have a feeling
they might come in handy."

"His bi*noc*ulars? Me-el. How long do you plan to stay
here? And what am I supposed to tell your parents if they
ask where you are?"

"Tell them the truth. Tell them I'm on the beach."

"Well . . . okay."

"Thanks, Lacey."

"You're welcome. I guess. See you later."

"'Bye." Mel trained her eyes on the house, and Lacey
retreated down the beach. After a while, as the bright-
ening sun reflected itself in the windows, Mel had to
shield her eyes against the glare.

She watched and watched, but nothing happened. Police stakeouts must be incredibly boring, she thought.

She wished she had her watch. She wished she had her
tape player.

The sun rose a bit higher, and Mel removed her sweat
shirt.

She was just beginning to feel slightly drowsy when
she caught a flicker of movement on the highest deck of
the house. Mel sprang to attention. A door slid open and
the boy stepped out. He was wearing blue bathing trunks,
the same ones he'd had on the first time Mel had seen
him. That's no coincidence, she thought. It's fate; it's
kismet.

A dark-haired woman wearing a white dress, or maybe
it was a white uniform, followed the boy onto the deck.
She was carrying a tray.

The boy sat down in a lounge chair and the woman

placed the tray on his lap. Then she sat on a bench near him, crossed her legs, and watched him eat.

Mel strained her eyes until they stung, but for the life of her, she couldn't make out what the boy was eating. She was still trying to see, when suddenly a pair of binoculars was thrust in front of her.

She looked up, blinking. "Thanks, Lace."

"Candidate for the loony bin," Lacey muttered. But she dropped a bag containing an orange, a hard-boiled egg, and a muffin onto the sand next to Mel before she left again, so Mel knew she wasn't really angry.

Mel was starving, but first things first. She wanted to get a good look at the scene on the deck before the woman and the boy left. She aimed the binoculars at the sun deck and adjusted the focus.

The result was more than she had hoped for. There was the boy, his handsome face looking pleasant but serious as he talked with the woman. Mel zeroed in on the tray in his lap. Nothing. The plate was empty except for a crumpled napkin.

She shifted to the right for a look at the woman. Curly brown hair. Dark, friendly eyes. Yes, the white dress was definitely a uniform. Perhaps she was a housekeeper.

A few moments later, the woman rose and picked up the empty tray. She carried it inside the house. The boy rose, too, and walked to the edge of the deck, where he rested his arms on the rail and gazed out to sea.

Hastily, Mel lowered the binoculars. She scrunched down in the sand, hoping the dunes hid her from the boy. When she dared to peep up again, he was gone.

Mel sighed. She raised the binoculars and scanned every inch of the house. She was halfway through counting the windows when a hand was suddenly clapped over the binoculars, blocking her view.

Mel shrieked and dropped the binoculars in the sand. She looked up.

The boy was standing over her.

Chapter Four

"What are you doing?" the boy demanded.

Mel paused. "Bird-watching?"

The boy's stern face almost relaxed into a smile. "I was watching you," he said. "From the deck. And you were watching me. Or the house. Although I can't figure out why you would want to watch my house."

"No, honest," said Mel. "There are great birds here. I saw a—a flamingo and a loon and twelve robins. Oh, and a sea gull."

The boy finally smiled—the same friendly grin that Mel had fallen in love with.

"Do I know you?" he asked suddenly.

Mel blushed. She'd hoped he would remember her. "We met once before. On the beach. My brother hit you with the Frisbee...?"

"Oh! Yes."

"Are you all right?"

"I'm fine. Just had a little bump for a few days. No big deal. Didn't even leave a bruise."

Mel looked at his perfect face and was unreasonably glad that the Frisbee hadn't flawed it in any way.

The boy dropped down in the sand beside her, hugged his knees to his chest, and looked out at the sea.

"You haven't been in Davis Park very long, have you?" said Mel.

"How could you tell?" The boy turned away from the ocean and fixed Mel with his brown eyes.

Mel could think of only one word to describe those eyes. It was a word she had come across in a book she'd read in English class that spring, and it was one of those words she'd thought you only *read* but would never actually have the occasion to *use*. Yet there she was, using it, or at least thinking it. The boy's eyes were *limpid*. They were like deep, clear pools of water. Mel was sure they indicated great sensitivity.

"How could you tell?" the boy asked again.

"Oh," said Mel. "Well, for one thing, you didn't know what Bedside Manor is."

The boy smiled. "I do now, though. I asked my father about it that night."

"Your father," Mel repeated. "He's been here before?"

"Just for the rest of this summer. I've been . . . busy this summer. This is the first chance I've had to come out to his house."

Mel looked over her shoulder at the rambling beach

house. "Did your father just buy it?"

"Oh, no. He's renting it. Usually he rents a place in
Southampton, but this summer he wanted to try something
new. What about you? How long have you been here?"

"Since as soon as school let out. And before that, every
weekend that the weather was nice. We own a house.
I've been spending summers here my entire life. Mom
and Dad had the house before they had me, even before
they had Dee—she's my older sister. I think the house
is like their first child."

The boy laughed.

Mel laughed too and stretched her legs out in front of
her, suddenly self-conscious. She hoped she wasn't talking too much. She wondered if she was acting the way
you're supposed to act the first time you talk to a boy
you like. She wondered if Dee would handle things dif-
ferently. After all, Dee had had a lot more experience
than Mel. Then Mel wondered how it was even possible
to like someone you'd barely met. For all Mel knew, the
boy was an ax murderer.

No, she thought, not with those *limpid* eyes. It was
not possible.

Conversation had lagged. Mel wanted to start it up
again, but she wasn't sure what to say. She was also
starving, and was dying to open the bag that Lacey had
brought her, but she knew she'd be embarrassed to eat
in front of the boy. And, thanks to her spying, she knew
he'd already eaten and probably wouldn't want to share
her breakfast.

Finally, however, the food won out. Mel felt that her

stomach was about to rumble and decided she'd rather do almost anything than rumble in front of the boy. She opened the bag and took out the muffin.

"Want half?" she asked, just to be polite.

"Sure," replied the boy.

Pleased, Mel broke the muffin in two and handed him a piece.

"Thanks," he said. He peered in the bag. "What are those? Provisions?"

Mel giggled. "I was prepared for a long stay."

The boy shook his head, smiling. "How did you know where I live?"

"Oh, I didn't," said Mel. "My friend—Lacey, the one who was with me when Timmy hit you—she and I were watching the sunrise on the beach. It was the first time in fourteen summers that we actually got up early enough to see it. Anyway, when it was over, I saw you, and then I began watching you instead. When you walked back here, I sort of followed you."

Mel and the boy had finished the muffin. Mel took the orange out of the bag and began to peel it.

"Where are you from?" asked the boy. "I mean, aside from down the beach."

"Bronxville," Mel replied. "My dad works in New York City, but he and Mom don't want to raise kids in the city, so Dad commutes from the suburbs. I wish they did want to raise us in New York. It's my favorite place in the whole world, next to Fire Island. My friend Lacey lives in New York. She's so lucky."

"I live there, too," said the boy.

"Really?" asked Mel with interest. "Where?"

"It depends."

"On what?"

"On whether I'm at my dad's apartment or my mother's."

"Oh," said Mel knowingly. So his parents were divorced.

The boy found a piece of shell in the sand and began tracing patterns with it, moving it back and forth, back and forth.

"How long have your parents been divorced?" asked Mel.

"Forever," replied the boy. "I don't even remember a time when the three of us lived together."

"You don't have any brothers or sisters?"

The boy shook his head. "Not unless you count Rochelle."

"Rochelle?"

"My mom's collie."

"Your mother has a dog named Ro*chelle?*" Mel began to giggle.

The boy smiled. "She says it's her favorite girl's name, and she's not going to have any more children, so she might as well use it on the dog."

"Your mother sounds funny."

"She is. Actually, she's kind of wild. I go back and forth between my mom's place and my dad's. You know, equal time. When I'm at my mom's, I hardly ever see her. She's always off doing things—going to big parties, taking hula lessons, spending the weekend on someone's yacht. Once she tried skydiving. Do you know the story of *Mame*?"

Mel nodded.

"My mother is kind of like Auntie Mame."

"*Oh,*" said Mel, impressed. "Wow. What about your dad?"

"He's great, but he works really hard. I don't see that much of him either. He's a movie director."

"You're kidding!" exclaimed Mel.

"Yeah. Right now he's working on a movie in California. He's been back and forth, back and forth all summer."

"What do you do when it's your dad's turn to have you and he's out in California?"

"You sure ask a lot of questions," the boy said cheerfully.

"Sorry. I can't help it. It's just part of me. Maybe I'll put it to good use and become a newspaper reporter some day."

For a moment, the boy didn't say anything. Then he answered Mel's question. "Well, anyway, when Dad's gone, his housekeeper stays with me. Leila. She's okay. She's here now. She's been back and forth too, between the apartment and this house all summer, trying to take care of both places and keep an eye on me, too."

Mel tried to imagine what it would be like to have as much money as this boy's family seemed to have. She tried to imagine how she would feel if her parents were divorced and she had two families instead of just one. She decided it might be glamorous and exciting for about a week, and then she would be glad to be back in one snug, housekeeperless home with *both* her parents.

The boy stood up. "I've practically told you my life history," he said. "Let's walk to the Casino, and then you can tell me about *you.*"

"So you know the Casino."

"It's hard to miss. Besides, Dad took me there for dinner on Thursday night."

The Casino was the restaurant on the beach. It was also the gathering spot for all of Davis Park. Next to the restaurant was a room with a bar and video games where people went dancing at night. Outside the building were benches and soda machines, and a counter for ordering hot dogs, hamburgers and French fries.

Mel stood up and dusted the sand off her legs. She tossed the remains of her breakfast in a trash can, and she and the boy headed down the beach.

"So? What about you?" asked the boy as they walked slowly through the sand.

"There's not much to tell," replied Mel. "There's my mom and my dad and me, and my sister Dee—she's sixteen—and Timmy the Frisbee-thrower—he's nine."

"And Lacey?"

"Lacey Reeder's my summertime best friend. Her family's beach house is next door to ours. We've spent every summer of our lives together. But since the Reeders live in New York City, I don't see her much the rest of the year."

The boy nodded.

He and Mel ambled down the beach, which was filling

up quickly. It must be almost lunchtime, Mel realized.

They reached the Casino and sat down on one of the benches, facing the ocean.

"What do you want?" asked the boy. "Coke? Diet Coke?"

"Mel! Hey, Mel!" a voice called suddenly. Timmy came flying up the wooden steps to the Casino. "I've been looking for you everywhere. Mom wants you to come home. She says, 'Have you forgotten we're having a lobster picnic since Dad's here?' Come on!"

Mel, her cheeks burning, looked forlornly at the boy. "I guess I better go. Sorry."

"Hey, that's okay," he replied. "Look, I'll see you around."

"Really?"

"Really."

"Mel, come *on*." Timmy had grabbed her hand.

"Okay, okay," said Mel crossly. She followed her brother down the steps, pausing once to turn and wave to the boy. It wasn't until she was halfway home that Mel realized she still didn't know the boy's name.

Chapter Five

Mel couldn't believe she'd been so stupid as not to get the boy's name or give him hers. He didn't even know where she lived. What if she never saw him again? Immediately, she realized that that was silly because *she* knew where *he* lived, and if she didn't see him in a few days, she could always go to his house.

Then she began to worry. First she worried that the boy, in thinking the morning over, would decide she'd been too pushy—following him down the beach and spying on his house. Then she worried that he'd think she didn't really like him—after all, she hadn't told him her name.

Mel spent the afternoon wondering what to do. She barely tasted her lobster and was too preoccupied to talk to her father (or anyone else). After supper that evening, she decided she needed to be alone to think.

"I'm going to the ferry dock," she announced. She threw on her sneakers and ran down the walk. Then she slap-slapped along through the dusk to the boats. One look up the ferry dock showed her that too many people were already there to allow any privacy. She strolled a bit further to the last dock in the bay and walked all the way out to the end.

There she plopped down, her feet hanging over the side. They didn't quite reach the water. She leaned back on her hands and gazed across the bay. Very faintly, she could see the mainland along the horizon. The sun, a glowing orange orb, had set several minutes earlier.

Mel kicked her feet back and forth and thought.

She closed her eyes, feeling the damp, salty breeze on her face, and tried to picture the boy—his limpid eyes, his head of curls. After a few moments, she sensed that someone had sat down beside her. Inwardly, she groaned. She had come to the dock to be alone. Who had followed her? Lacey? Dee? Timmy?

Finally she opened her eyes and looked around.

It was the boy!

"Hi!" Mel cried.

"Hello," said the boy. "I thought it was you. I was taking a walk and I saw you from the Harbor Store."

"I needed a little peace and quiet."

"Do you want me to leave?"

"Oh, no!" said Mel quickly. "No, I want you to stay."
Immediately, she wondered whether she was being too

forward again. "I mean, if you want to stay."

"Sure," the boy replied. "You know, I love the sun, and lying around on the beach, but I think this is my favorite time of day."

"Mine, too," said Mel. "Or maybe a little later than this. I kind of like the dark. I used to be afraid of it, but now I like it. Timmy says I'm weird. I like rain, too."

"You do? So do I! I like sitting by a window with the rain streaming down the panes."

"When I was little, my mom used to read this poem to me. It's called 'Windy Nights,' but the first four lines are about rain, and I love them."

"I know what they are," the boy said. "'Whenever the moon and stars are set, Whenever the wind is high, All night long in the dark and wet'—"

"'A man goes riding by,'" Mel finished. "Robert Louis Stevenson. . . . 'In the dark and wet,'" she said again. "I love those words. Who used to read to you? Your dad?"

The boy shook his head.

"Oh, your mom, then."

He shook his head again. "Leila. Leila read to me all the time."

"Oh."

Mel and the boy looked out across the bay. On the mainland, lights twinkled here and there, some shining alone, some in friendly clusters.

"So what have you been doing this summer?" Mel asked, remembering that the boy had said he'd been busy before he left for Fire Island.

"Just working."

Mel nodded. She was incredibly glad that his work was finished.

"You still haven't told me very much about yourself," the boy said, changing the subject. "I know about Dee and Timmy and Lacey, but not you."

Mel gave the boy a wry smile. "The first thing to know about me is that my name is Melanie Braderman. Everyone calls me Mel, though, except the woman who used to baby-sit for me, and she calls me Melly. No one else is allowed to." Mel paused.

The boy didn't say anything.

"So is your name a secret or what?" asked Mel. "I mean, do I have to guess it? You're not Rumpelstiltskin, are you?"

The boy laughed. "My name is Justin."

"Justin what? Justin Time?"

"Justin Hart." He was still laughing.

"Well, anyway, Justin Hart, I'm fourteen and I'm going to be a freshman at Bronxville High School this fall. And I'm scared to death."

"Scared to death? Of what?"

"Upperclassmen."

"Why?"

"Well, for starters—Freshman Torture Day."

Justin looked shocked. "What," he asked, "is Freshman Torture Day?"

"To be honest," said Mel, "I'm not positive it's anything. Dee swears up and down that there's no such thing. I've heard so many rumors, though. The kids in seventh and eighth grade are always telling stories about their older brothers and sisters coming home from their first day at BHS with big *F*'s written on their foreheads in red lipstick, and having to be the seniors' slaves. Things like that."

"Well," said Justin practically, "what happened to Dee on her first day at BHS?"

"Nothing."

"See?"

"No, it doesn't prove a thing. Dee is gorgeous. Upper-class boys don't want to torture her; they want to date her. I, on the other hand, am just the kind of person a sophomore boy would rather haze than kiss."

"Sweet sixteen and only been hazed?"

Mel giggled. "Always a hazee, never a date."

They were both laughing.

"I'm an upperclassman, and I wouldn't want to haze you," said Justin.

Mel gulped. For some reason, she had assumed that she and Justin were the same age. "How old are you?"

"Oh, old. As old as the hills."

"No, really."

"Fifteen," replied Justin. "I'm going to be a great big menacing sophomore."

"Where do you go to school?" asked Mel.

"It's a private school," Justin said vaguely.

"Really? Is it Ethical Culture? That's where Lacey goes."

"No, not Ethical Culture. You probably haven't heard of it."

"Probably not," agreed Mel.

"Listen," said Justin. "Would you like to walk to Watch Hill tomorrow evening?"

"Sure!" replied Mel.

"Great. I was thinking we could get ice cream or something at the restaurant there. And if we time it right, we could watch the sunset on the way."

"Oh, that sounds perfect." Mel could hardly believe it! Justin Hart, the boy she had been spying on just that morning, was asking her for a *date*. Anyway, it was as close to a date as she had ever come.

"Where should we meet?" asked Justin.

"At the Casino?"

"Okay. I'll wait for you by the soda machines at seven o'clock." Justin stood up. "I really should be getting back. I told Leila I wouldn't be gone long, and I hate to make her worry."

"I should probably go, too." Mel took one last look at the bay and got to her feet. She and Justin walked back along the dock. Justin, she noticed, was exactly as tall as she was. She matched her stride to his and walked just close enough to him so that their shoulders and elbows touched lightly.

At the end of the dock they separated. "See you tomorrow!" Mel called.

Justin grinned. "Seven o'clock!"

Mel walked sedately along the boardwalk in front of the Harbor Store. After a few moments, she looked over her shoulder. Justin had already disappeared. Mel broke into a frantic run and tore home.

"Mom! Mom!" she cried as she burst through the front door of Moonrise House.

"Melanie? What is it?" Mrs. Braderman stepped out of the bedroom, looking worried.

"It's great news! Oh, I can't believe it!" Mel collapsed on the couch, hugging herself with joy.

"Well, what? Tell me."

Mel sat up and patted the couch next to her.

Mrs. Braderman took a seat. "Do you want your father to hear this news, too?"

"Sure," replied Mel.

"Honey!" Mrs. Braderman called. "Come here for a sec. Mel has some news."

Mel's father joined them on the couch.

"Okay, here goes I . . .," said Mel, trying to drag out the suspense (her father looked at his watch), "have a date tomorrow night."

"A date? With a *boy?*" asked Mr. Braderman.

"Of course with a boy."

"Honey, that's wonderful," said her mother. "Do we know this boy?"

"No, not really. His name is Justin Hart. Oh, Mom, he's so cute. And nice. I really like him."

"Where's he taking you on the date?" her father wanted to know.

"We're going to walk to Watch Hill at sunset."

"Hmm. Are your mother and I going to meet him first?"

"Probably not. He's just going to wait for me in front of the Casino."

"Well . . ."

"Dad, what is it?"

"I'd kind of like to see what he's like before you go off on a date with him. Where did you meet him?"

"On the beach. I think he's shy, Dad," said Mel. "Besides, what are you worried about? We'll walk through the wildlife preserve. A lot of people will be around at that hour. We won't be alone for a second. I can go, can't I? You're not going to deprive me of my very first date . . . are you?"

Mel's parents looked at each other. They shrugged. "I don't see why you can't go," her father said at last.

Mel grinned. "Thanks, Dad."

Mrs. Braderman hugged her. "Honey, I'm so happy for you."

"Me, too," said Mel. "I'm *very* happy for me. "

Chapter Six

"You know," said Mel, "it's funny. Your first date is kind of like your birthday or a big holiday. You think about it and plan for it and dream about it, and then all of a sudden—boom, it happens. It's right there. You think your birthday will never come—and suddenly it's over.

"I've been dreaming about getting asked out on a date ever since Dee started dreaming about it. And then last night Justin asks me, and now, in twenty minutes, it will start, and in a couple of hours it will be over. I can't believe it."

"Mmm."

Mel glanced at Lacey, who was perched on the Bradermans' deck railing. They'd been sitting on the deck for fifteen minutes, and, if "Mmm" counted as a word, then

Lacey had spoken exactly two words since she'd come over. The other word had been "Hi."

"Is anything wrong?" Mel asked.

Lacey shook her head. She was wearing an outfit Mel would have died for. It was a typical Lacey outfit—a hot-pink T-shirt under a cotton jumpsuit made from a wildflower print. Mel considered her own outfit, which was typically Mel. She was wearing baggy jeans, new sneakers, and a sweat shirt that said "If God had wanted me to cook, he wouldn't have invented restaurants."

"Do you think I should change?" Mel asked Lacey.

"Oh, *could* you?" asked a voice from inside the house. "Could you change into a cow?"

"Shut up, Timmy," said Mel. "Lacey, really," she went on. "This sweat shirt is funny, but maybe it's not right for a first date. Could I borrow your other jumpsuit? The one with the star bursts all over it?"

Lacey looked at her watch, then at Mel. "You don't have time," she replied. "Besides, you look fine."

"Not as good as you."

"Well, I don't see what you're worried about. You got a date, didn't you?" Lacey snapped. "He met you in the dunes spying on his house with binoculars, carrying a bag with a hard-boiled egg in it, and wearing your most disgusting sweat shirt, and he still asked you to go to Watch Hill with him. What are you worried about?"

Mel frowned at Lacey. "I don't know. . . . Are you sure nothing's wrong?"

"Positive."

"I know it's Sunday, and we usually see our dads off

on the ferry, but—well, look, I might get back in time
to see them off anyway, if Justin and I don't stay too
long, and if our fathers take the late ferry—"

"I said nothing was wrong."

"Okay, okay. . . . Well, I guess I better go meet Justin."
Lacey slid off the railing. "Have fun," she said, and
ran down the Bradermans' walk and up the next one to
Starfish House.

Mel watched her, puzzled. Then she stuck her head
into her own house and called, "'Bye, everybody. I'm
going."

"'Bye, sweetie. Have fun," said her mother.

"Come here and give me a kiss," said her father. "I'll
be gone by the time you get back."

Mel ran inside. "Have a good week, Dad. See you
Thursday." Then she headed back out.

Dee raised her eyebrows. "Don't do anything I wouldn't
do," she said, grinning.

Timmy didn't say a word. He simply wrapped his arms
around himself and made loud kissing noises.

Mel stuck her tongue out at him and left the house.
She jogged along the walks to the Casino, wondering and
worrying every step of the way. Was she dressed properly?
Was she supposed to pay for her own ice cream? (She'd
brought some money, in case.) Would they find enough
things to talk about?

But as soon as she saw Justin leaning against a soda
machine waiting for her, she knew she had no reason to
worry.

"Hi!" she called to him.

He waved to her, smiling.

Mel jogged up to him, and he stepped back to read her T-shirt. Then he laughed. "Pretty funny," he said. "I like T-shirts. I have a collection."

"You do?"

"Yeah. I save the ones with pictures or slogans that I like."

They set off along the boardwalk that would lead them through the wildlife preserve to the restaurant at Watch Hill.

"What's your favorite?" asked Mel. "Do you have one?"

"Sure, but I can only wear it when I'm with my father. He gave it to me, and it's part of a set. He has to wear the other one. Mine has an arrow pointing to the left and says, 'I'm his kid.' Dad's has an arrow pointing to the right and says, 'I'm his dad.' We always have to walk in the same positions when we wear them. Otherwise, we'd point to strangers."

Mel laughed. "My grandparents once gave me a T-shirt that said 'Grandma and Grandpa went to Florida and all they brought me was this dumb T-shirt.' I was too embarrassed to wear it."

"I don't blame you."

Mel and Justin ambled along the walk through the preserve. They listened to the sounds of the birds settling down for the night. They looked west and realized that the sunset would be blocked by a bank of clouds. Every now and then a couple or a family would pass them in the other direction.

"Half the parents here have to leave tonight," Mel commented. "My father will be gone when I get home."

"My father's been away, but he's coming back again," said Justin. "But I won't see him."

"You won't? Why not?"

"I'll explain later."

They walked the rest of the way to Watch Hill in peaceful silence.

When they were seated at an outdoor table at the restaurant, Justin said, "I know what I want—a hot fudge sundae. How about you? What do you want? Do you have a sweet tooth?"

"Do I have a sweet tooth?" repeated Mel. "I could probably recite the ingredients on any package of junk food you handed me—Yodels, Ring-Dings, Ding-Dongs, Twinkies, fruit pies. . . . You name it—I know it, love it, and eat it. I'll have a butterscotch sundae. It's the sweetest thing I can think of."

Justin grinned. Then he gave their order to a waitress. While they waited for their food, they peeled the ends off the wrappers on their straws and blew the papers at each other.

The sundaes arrived and they dug in. Justin chose the moment that Mel was about to pop the maraschino cherry into her mouth to drop his bombshell. "You know," he said, "I've only known you for two days, but it feels like a lot longer."

"Yeah," said Mel, "at least three days." (She hadn't gotten to the cherry yet and was scooping the whipped cream up around the edge of her dish.)

Justin smiled. "I wish it didn't feel so long."

Mel felt something tear inside her. "Why?" she whispered, still absent-mindedly working on the whipped cream.

"Because it's going to be so hard to leave."

That was when Mel popped the cherry in her mouth. She sat there for several seconds, unable to chew it. "What do you mean?" she finally asked, tucking the cherry into her cheek like a hamster. "We've got three weeks before Labor Day."

Justin nodded. "But I have to leave tomorrow."

"Tomorrow!" Mel exclaimed, stricken.

"Not for good, just for a week."

"Still," said Mel, "a week is a week. When you come back, we'll only have two weeks until we have to leave the island. That is, if you're staying until the end of the summer."

"We are."

"Well, that's something. Where are you going tomorrow?" She managed to swallow the cherry.

"Back to New York."

"Why?"

"Just have to finish up my work."

"Your work. What do you do? What's so important that you have to leave Fire Island for a week?"

"It's hard to explain, but look, I'll be back next Saturday, on the earliest ferry I can get."

"Promise?"

"Promise. Have I ever let you down?"

"No. Not once in the entire thirty-five hours we've known each other."

They finished their sundaes, and the waitress brought the bill. There was a little scuffle over who would pay it. The waitress had handed it to Justin, who immediately pulled his wallet out of his pocket. At the same time, Mel took her money out of the pocket of her jeans.

"I'll pay," Justin said.

"I'll help," Lacey replied. "Boys shouldn't have to pay for everything."

"But *I* asked *you* out, so this is *my* treat. You can pay next time."

"Okay. Thanks." Mel gave in, not wanting an argument. She put her money away. Anyway, all she could think of was that Justin had said "next time." That meant he wanted to go out with her again!

They held hands as they walked back through the wildlife preserve to Davis Park. Mel decided that she had never, ever been happier than she was at that moment.

When they reached the Casino, they separated. "I'll see you on Saturday," said Justin.

"Promise?" Mel asked again.

"Promise. Meet the eight-thirty ferry. I'll be on it."

"Okay. . . . Good-bye, Justin."

"'Bye, Mel."

Mel watched him disappear into the twilight. Then she walked slowly to Moonrise House. As she started up her walk, she noticed Lacey sitting alone on the deck next door. Mel turned and headed for Starfish House instead.

"Hi!" she called softly. "Where is everybody?"

"Over at your house."

"Oh, good. Lacey, I have to tell you everything! Tonight was *won*derful!"

"I'm busy," replied Lacey. She was sitting in a lounge chair without so much as a magazine in her hands.

"Busy doing what? It's dark out here."

"I'm thinking."

"But Lacey, tonight—"

"Mel, excuse me, but I really couldn't care less. And please don't think you can use me this way."

"Use you!" exclaimed Mel, confused. "Use you what way?"

"You go off with Justin whenever you feel like it, and then you expect to come back and find me just waiting for you. Like you can squeeze me in around the edges of Justin, whenever it's convenient for the two of you. Well, did it occur to you that I might have things to do? I might be busy, too."

"Lacey," Mel said slowly, "if I didn't know better, I'd think you were jealous."

"Then apparently you *don't* know better. Of course I'm jealous. You're changing things. Our summers aren't supposed to include boys. You're spoiling everything." Lacey's chin began to tremble.

Mel pretended not to notice. "Well, thanks a *lot.* That's a nice thing to say. I thought you'd be happy for me, but I can see that you're too immature for that." Mel stomped down the boardwalk and decided to take a moonlight walk in order to cool off before she went home.

She and Lacey didn't speak for three days.

Chapter Seven

"Okay, Mel, your turn. 'What gooey toy was sold in a plastic egg?'"

"Oh, easy," Mel replied. "Silly Putty. We used to have some. Remember, Dee? But Mom and Dad made us throw it out after we left it on the chair in the living room and Dad sat on it and ruined his plaid bathrobe."

Dee and Jeanmarie laughed. "You're on a roll, kid," said Dee. "Go again."

Mel rolled the dice and moved her piece around the Trivia Chase board. "All right." She sighed. "This is for a piece of the pie. Hit me with an arts and literature question."

Jeanmarie withdrew a card from one of the boxes. "'Who wrote *The Hunchback of Notre Dame*?'"

"Oh, thank goodness. Another easy one. Victor Hugo."

Jeanmarie turned the card over and checked the answer. "She's right!" she said to Dee. "How does she know all this stuff?"

"All she does is read."

Mel rolled again. "All right. I just need the geography piece and my pie will be full."

Mel was ahead of both older girls, which pleased her, but, quite truthfully, she was bored. And anxious. It was Tuesday afternoon. It had been raining since Monday morning, and Lacey hadn't spoken to Mel since Sunday evening. Mel was glad for the company of Dee and Jeanmarie, but she missed Lacey, and Justin as well. Besides, she felt as if she'd been playing Trivia Chase for two solid years, instead of just off and on for two days.

When Mel finally missed a question, she leaned back against the sofa and closed her eyes.

"Everything all right?" her sister asked.

"I guess."

"We know you and Lacey had a fight," said Jeanmarie. "Lacey can be pretty stubborn. Just ignore her. She'll come to her senses."

"It's hard to ignore her. She's my best friend."

"Well," said Dee, "things always work out."

"No, they don't," replied Mel soberly. "They really don't. Not always. People have fights and never make up. People move away and say, 'I'll write,' and never do. People go away and say, 'I'll come back,' and never do."

"Those are cheery thoughts," said Dee.

Mel sighed. "I think I'll take a walk."

"Oh, come on. It's pouring out there. At least finish the game. I'm about to catch up with you." Dee rolled the dice gleefully.

So Mel finished the game, beating Dee and Jeanmarie, and then put on her slicker and headed to the beach for a barefoot, misty walk. She reached the dunes, turned right, and trudged through the damp sand, the wind and spray in her face, the cold gray water biting her feet.

Words were funny, she thought. If the weather were nice and the ocean blue, she would probably imagine that the water was kissing her feet, not biting them.

She walked alone along the water's edge until she realized she was standing opposite Justin's house. She could barely see it through the mist and rain, but there it was. For some reason, Mel felt comforted by the sight of it, even though she knew Justin wasn't in it.

She stared at it for several moments, jumping slightly when a light was switched on in a second-story room. Then she turned and walked back to Moonrise House.

Trivia Chase was still going on. Dee and Jeanmarie had been joined by Timmy, Jackie, Mrs. Braderman, and Mrs. Reeder. They were playing on teams, the Bradermans versus the Reeders.

"Come on and join us, honey," Mel's mother said as Mel hung up her dripping coat.

"Thanks, Mom, but then your teams would be uneven."

"Well, go get Lacey," suggested Mrs. Reeder. "She's been moping around since the rain started."

Mel shook her head. "No, thanks. I think I'll do some writing."

She saw her mother and Mrs. Reeder exchange knowing looks as she headed for the bedroom.

Once in the bedroom, Mel picked up her journal and
decided to write some poetry. She turned to a blank page,
put the end of her pen in her mouth, and sat thoughtfully.
After several minutes she wrote:

> Blackbird, fly away.

Then she crossed it out.

She wrote:

> Violet petals on the wind.

She crossed that out, too.

She wrote:

> Good-bye, Lacey.
> Good-bye, Fire Island.

That was very depressing, but she didn't cross it out.
Instead, she closed her journal with a snap, lay down on
her bed, fell sound asleep, and dreamed one of the oddest
dreams she could remember having.

In the beginning of the dream, she was walking along
the beach in the mist, the water biting her toes. Only it
actually hurt, and after a while, Mel realized she ought
to stay away from it. She kept moving farther and farther
back toward the dunes, but the water drew farther and
farther up as the tide came in.

"Stay away!" Mel cried.

The biting water turned into thousands of pairs of chattering teeth, the kind sold in joke shops. The teeth had
minds of their own, and clickety-clacked after her as she
ran up a flight of wooden steps and along a boardwalk.
She had to find Justin, and she ran right to his house,

but when she reached the back door, she realized it was Starfish House instead. Lacey slammed the door in Mel's face.

"Let me in!" shouted Mel. "Let me in!"

Something was shaking her shoulder. Oh, no, Mel thought. What now? What's behind me? "Go away!"

"It's dinnertime."

"Go away!"

"Mel, come *on*. Dinner."

Mel woke up with a start to find Dee bending over her. "Come on," she said again. "It's six-thirty. You've been asleep for two hours."

Mel groaned. "I don't feel well. I'm not hungry."

She slept fitfully that night, but by the next morning seemed to have recovered.

So had the weather.

Mel awoke to a clear, cloudless, brilliantly sunny sky. She raced to the beach and spent the better part of the day there.

Lacey studiously ignored her all morning and afternoon, but that evening she came over to Moonrise House just as Mel was heading out for the ice-cream stand.

Mel couldn't imagine why she had come over. "Jackie's not here," she said. "He and Timmy went to the bay."

Lacey looked at the ground. "I didn't come for Jackie. I came to see you."

"Me? The summer spoilsport? The one who's using you?"

"Mel, I came to apologize. I'm really sorry I said all

those things. I didn't mean them. Well, maybe I thought
I did at the time, but I didn't really. I mean . . . Oh, you
know what I mean. I'm sorry."

Mel smiled. "Want to go get ice cream?"

Lacey pulled a dollar bill out of the pocket of her sweat
pants. "I was hoping you'd ask. I came prepared."

The girls bought their cones at the stand, then walked
out to the end of one of the docks in the bay. It was the
same dock where Justin had found Mel four nights earlier,
but Mel didn't tell Lacey that.

They sat on the end, their feet hanging over the side,
and licked at their cones. "You know what's funny?" said
Mel. "I'm fourteen and you're fourteen, but you've always seemed older than me. More sophisticated, I guess.
You look older, too."

"So?" Lacey prompted her.

"So isn't it funny that I'd be the first one of us to find
a boyfr—a boy I like?"

Lacey looked at her wavery reflection in the lapping
water. "Yeah."

"Have you ever liked a boy?" asked Mel.

"I don't know."

"How can you not know?"

Lacey shrugged. "I just don't know."

"Well, have you ever been interested in a boy?"

"I don't really want to talk about this, okay?"

Mel took a long look at Lacey, who sat with her head
bent, toying with the remainder of her ice-cream cone.
"Hey, Lacey, you're not afraid of boys, are you?"

Another shrug. "It's not so much that I'm afraid of

them. It's more that I'm afraid they won't like me."

"How could anyone not like you?"

"Oh, Mel, that is such a *mother* thing to say. Talk to me as a friend, not as a mother. One mother is enough. You know perfectly well how someone could not like me."

"But you're so sophisticated. I mean, you dress the same way in New York that you do here, don't you? And I just wear jeans and sweats and stuff, and Justin likes me."

"Somehow I think there's more to it than that. You know how to talk to people, which I guess includes boy-people. And I don't. . . . Do you think Justin is going to change us?"

"Change you and me?" asked Mel. "Well—"

"I mean, boys were bound to come up sometime. And I suppose one of us was bound to be ready for them before the other one. . . ."

"It's not easy," said Mel slowly. "And I guess maybe Justin—or whoever—*will* change things between us. But we'll always be friends, won't we?"

"Oh, I hope so," Lacey said, finally turning to look at Mel. "I hope so."

Chapter Eight

Mel was up at the crack of dawn on Saturday morning. She was bound and determined to meet the ferry Justin would be on, and not look sleepy. In fact, the night before, at Mel's insistence, Dee had given her a crash course in makeup, and Mel methodically applied blusher, mascara, and eyeliner before she left Moonrise House.

She reached the ferry dock ten minutes before the boat was due in, and sat on a wooden bench, straining her eyes across the bay for the first glimpse of the *Kiki*. At last she could see it, moving slowly through the gray water. It chugged toward the island, motor roaring, until it reached the markers a little distance from the dock. Then the motor was cut and the boat purred in lazily.

Mel spotted Justin on a seat on the upper deck. She

waved madly to him, and when he saw her, he waved back, grinning broadly. A few seconds later, he disappeared. When the gangplank was lowered, Justin was the first one off the *Kiki*.

He ran to Mel. "Hi!" he cried.

"Hi! I missed you!"

"Same here."

"Is that all your stuff?"

Justin was carrying a duffel bag in one hand and a knapsack in the other. "Yeah, that's it. I travel light."

They ambled to the end of the ferry dock. "It's early," said Mel. "What do you want to do?"

"Let's go to my house so I can dump my stuff off and tell Leila I'm here. Then do you want to take a walk on the beach? I could use a little exercise."

"Sure," replied Mel. "That sounds great." In the back of her mind, she was thinking that if Justin had asked her to come along and pick through trash at a dump, she would gladly have accompanied him.

They reached Justin's house, which Mel found out was named Dune House, and Mel waited outside while Justin went in with his bags. He had asked her in, and she had declined. She wasn't sure why, but she didn't feel like meeting Leila just then.

Justin returned presently, and he and Mel set off for the beach. Mel told him what had happened with Lacey.

"It works the other way, too," Justin said. "Sometimes girls come between guys."

"Has it ever happened to you?"

"No, but I've seen it happen to one or two of my friends. It started happening last year, when we were freshmen. It was no big deal, though."

"Something you'll look back on and laugh about?" asked Mel.

Justin smiled. "I guess so."

"Well," said Mel, "Lacey and I haven't laughed about our fight, but I think we saw that there wasn't that much to be fighting about in the first place. Neither of us did anything actually *wrong,* although I know Lacey felt hurt."

Justin nodded.

"Well, on to cheerier subjects," said Mel.

"So, besides having a fight with Lacey Reeder, what did you do while I was gone?"

"Played Trivia Chase till it came out my ears. I bet I know the answer to every single question on every single card. And I finished an Agatha Christie mystery and worked on a watercolor and wrote poetry in my journal. What did you do?"

"Nothing much," replied Justin vaguely. "You sure were busy. Do you always have so many projects going?"

"Usually. I don't know why. Dee once told me I act like someone who's been told she has only six months to live, and has to cram as much as possible into her remaining time. I've always been like that."

"Hey, Mel?" said Justin.

"Yeah?"

He paused. "Nothing."

But the next thing Mel knew, he had reached for her

hand and laced his fingers through hers. Mel's heart pounded. They walked up the beach in silence.

On Sunday, they didn't see each other. Mr. Braderman was on the island, of course, and Justin's father had flown in unexpectedly. Mel and Justin spent the day with their families.

On Monday afternoon, Justin took Mel clamming in the bay. Mel loathed clams—live or cooked—but she enjoyed clamming under the lowering sun with Justin.

On Tuesday evening, they walked to Watch Hill again. They saw four deer in the wildlife preserve. "If I were a deer, I'd be scared of us," commented Mel.

"I guess they're used to people," Justin replied. "Besides, if *I* were a deer, I wouldn't be scared of you."

He took her hand and they walked on.

Wednesday was a rainy day, so Mel stayed at home. The entire Reeder family came over just after lunch, and Mel, Lacey, Timmy, Jackie, Dee, Jeanmarie, Mrs. Braderman, and Mrs. Reeder began a vicious game of Monopoly. By the time Timmy won, four and a half hours later, he had cleaned out every player plus the bank, and the sun was shining palely.

Mel decided to find Justin. She ran along the damp walks, the wet trees dripping onto her skin, and nearly slammed into somebody as she rounded a corner.

"Justin!" she exclaimed.

"Mel! Where are you going?"

"To find you. The sun's out and I thought maybe we could take a walk."

"Oh, good. I was on my way to ask you the same thing."

Hand in hand, they walked to the beach. Neither one felt the need to speak. When they reached the steps down to the dunes, Mel paused. "Let's sit up here and look at the ocean," she said. "The sand is too wet to sit in."

They sat side by side on the top step, their shoulders touching. Justin took one of Mel's hands and held it between both of his. "A hand sandwich," commented Mel.

"You know what I've been thinking?" Justin said a few moments later.

"What?"

"That in less than two weeks, we'll have left the is-land."

"Yuck. I know," said Mel. "Back to school. We might come out for a few weekends in September, though. What about you?"

Justin shook his head. "We only have the house until the end of Labor Day weekend."

"Oh."

"And then I'll be back in New York."

"And I'll be back in Bronxville."

"How often do you get into the city?" asked Justin.

"Not very often. Maybe three or four times a year—to see the Reeders or go to a show or something. My mother doesn't like New York."

"We're not coming back, you know," said Justin abruptly.

"Not coming back? Oh, you mean not coming back here next summer?"

He shook his head. "Dad's thinking about going to Block Island. Or maybe back to the Hamptons. And my mother's moving to L.A. I might be out in California a lot from now on."

"Oh."

"We're really not going to see each other much after Labor Day."

"I guess not."

"That's why I was thinking that we should make the most of what's left of the summer—"

"Definitely."

"—and then not try to see each other again."

"What?" cried Mel.

"It would be too hard. You'll be starting high school. You'll want to go out with new guys. Believe me, they'll want to go out with you."

"You think so?"

"Yes, and we shouldn't be tied down to each other. It would be pointless since we'll probably never see each other again."

"I suppose," Mel said slowly. She stared down at the hand sandwich, willing herself not to cry.

And then, ever so slowly, Justin let go of her hand, drew her to him, and kissed her lightly on the lips. Mel was startled, then felt herself begin to tingle with pleasure.

She leaned forward and, just as tenderly, kissed Justin back.

"A summer romance," Mel whispered.

"Yes," replied Justin. "It will have to be just a summer romance."

Chapter Nine

Labor Day weekend arrived. Mel's father showed up on Wednesday night. "For the final fling of the summer," he said.

Mel felt happy and sad at the same time, although she had to admit that the feelings of sadness were greater than the feelings of happiness. Late Thursday afternoon she stood on her front deck and looked around, realizing that the leaves on the shrubs and trees were already beginning to turn slightly. And one bush, almost overnight, had become a fiery ball of red. In the distance, though, she could hear the ocean, and that was comforting because it was a summer sound.

Mel sat on the railing and did some fast calculating. Basically, there were four nights and three days left to her summer. Monday didn't count because it would be spent packing up, putting the house in order, and leaving the island. If the Bradermans returned for any September weekends, they would bring only overnight clothing with them.

There were a lot of things Mel wanted to do for the "last" time before Monday. Some she wanted to do with her family, some with Lacey, and some with Justin. She didn't think she would have time for everything.

Timmy ran up the walk to Moonrise, interrupting Mel's thoughts. He plopped down on a beach chair and smirked at his sister.

"Hey, squirt," said Mel. "What are you looking so smug about?"

"Da dum de-dum." Timmy hummed the tune to "The Wedding March." "Your boyfriend's on the way over."

Mel brightened, overlooking Timmy's humming. "He is?"

"Yup. I just passed him. He said he was coming over here. He's never done that before."

"He's shy," Mel replied. "I think."

"Who's shy?" called Lacey's voice from her deck. "Are you guys gossiping? I'll be right over."

Uh-oh, thought Mel. Lacey will have to face Justin.

Sure enough, Lacey had no sooner settled herself on the railing next to Mel than Justin strode up the walk, looking nervous but determined. "Hi, everybody!" he called.

"Well, I guess I'll be going," said Lacey.

"No, wait," said Justin uncomfortably. "I wanted to know if you—all of you—would like to come down the beach and play volleyball. There's a really good game going on right in front of my house, but they could use some more players."

"Hey, that would be fun!" said Mel.

"Yeah!" agreed Timmy.

"I don't know," said Lacey. "I'm not very good at volleyball."

"It doesn't matter. Nobody there is," Justin assured her. "They're just having fun."

"I'll go get Jackie," said Timmy. "He'll want to play, too."

"So are you coming?" Mel asked Lacey.

"Sure," she replied. "Why not?"

They played for over an hour, Mel, Lacey, and Jackie joining one team, Timmy and Justin joining the other. It wasn't a very serious game, everyone laughing and making mistakes. Twice, Mel found herself cheering for the other team when Justin made a good play.

After it was over, they flopped down in the sand. Mel could tell that Timmy liked Justin. Timmy would have appreciated a big brother, she thought.

Mel could also see Lacey warming up to Justin. Lacey agreed to that later as she and Mel were walking along the beach back to their houses, Timmy and Jackie trailing behind.

"He's not half bad," said Lacey.

"Is that the best you can do?" teased Mel.

"Oh, all right, he's nice. Really nice. And funny. I can see why you like him."

"Really?"

"Really."

"So you don't think I'm bonkers anymore?"

"Nah. . . . Cuckoo, yes. Deluded, yes. But not bonkers. No way."

On Friday, Mel and Justin walked to Watch Hill one last time and later went clamming one last time. On Saturday, the weather reports began predicting stormy weather for Sunday and Monday, so Saturday was Mel's Lacey Day—one last day baking in the sun on the beach. They ate both breakfast and lunch in the dunes.

"How about a seafood cookout tonight?" Mrs. Braderman asked Mel that afternoon. "We could send to the mainland for lobsters and fish and have a picnic supper tonight. You could ask Justin to join us."

"Really?" cried Mel. "Oh, Mom, that would be fantastic!"

"Why don't you go ask him now?" suggested her mother. "I need to know how much food to order."

"Okay. Want to come, Lacey?"

"No, thanks. I'll bake. See you later."

Mel ran along the water's edge. When she reached Justin's stretch of the beach, she was sweaty and out of breath. She scanned the beach for him, then looked at his house. She saw him sunning on one of the decks and ran a bit closer.

"Justin! Hey, Justin!" she shouted.

Justin sat up and shaded his eyes. "Mel?" he called.

She waved. "Yeah, it's me. I'm down here. Want to come over for dinner tonight? We're going to have a seafood cookout. My mom asked if you could come."

"Well . . . sure. Thanks!"

"Great. Seven o'clock, okay?"

"Okay. See you then. 'Bye!"

"'Bye!" Mel ran back to give her mother the good news.

Justin showed up at Moonrise House at exactly seven o'clock. He managed to look both casual and well dressed. He was wearing neatly pressed khaki shorts, a red-and-blue striped polo shirt, and running shoes with no socks. Mel noticed that he had tried unsuccessfully to tame his mass of curls, and decided that it didn't matter. She didn't see how a person could possibly notice anything other than those limpid brown eyes of his, anyway.

"Mom, Dad," said Mel as Justin entered the living room, "this is Justin Hart. Justin, these are my parents, Mr. and Mrs. Braderman. You know Timmy. Oh, and this is my sister, Dorothy."

"Dee," said Dee.

Justin shook hands with Mel's parents and said hello to Dee and Timmy.

"Well, let's go out on the back deck," suggested Mrs. Braderman. "It's much too nice an evening to sit around inside."

So Justin and the Bradermans sat around outside instead. Mel could tell that Justin was a big hit with her family, even if he did seem more reserved than when he was alone with Mel.

They ate grilled bluefish and lobster and corn on the

cob until they could barely move. Then Dee suggested a game of Trivia Chase, the women against the men. Thanks to Justin, who knew the answer to every single entertainment question, the men almost won. But the other team included Mel, so the women won after all.

When the game was over, Mr. Braderman said, "So you're leaving the island on Monday, Justin?"

Justin nodded. "Yes, sir."

"And will you be back next summer?"

"No, I'm afraid not. Dad's decided to rent somewhere else. He liked Fire Island, but he likes change, too. He's thinking of Block Island."

"Well, I hope we'll see you this year from time to time," said Mel's mother. "Bronxville isn't too far from the city, and we do visit the Reeders every now and then."

Justin smiled. Then he stood up. "I guess I should be getting back. Thanks for dinner. It was really great. I'm glad you asked me."

"Our pleasure."

Justin shook hands with Mel's parents and said good-bye to Timmy and Dee.

"I'll walk you partway," Mel told him, and followed him through the house and down the walk. When they were out of sight of Moonrise, Justin slipped his hand into Mel's.

"Will we see each other tomorrow?" asked Mel.

"I hope so," Justin replied, "but I'm not sure. Dad's here. And it's supposed to rain. But I'll see you Monday definitely. Even if it's just to say good-bye."

"To say good-bye," Mel repeated. "Justin, we don't have to, you know."

"Yes, we do. This is just a summer romance, remember? It has to be."

"I know. No strings attached."

"Because it'll never work out later."

"Okay." Mel nodded, trying to convince herself. "Okay."

She and Justin kissed briefly. Then they parted.

Just as the weather forecasters had predicted, Sunday dawned overcast and cool. Mel and her family sat around their house with the radio playing. Mrs. Braderman worked on her needlepoint; Mr. Braderman, Dee, and Mel plowed through the *New York Times;* and Timmy decided to bake brownies.

It wasn't until early afternoon that they heard the first warnings about Hurricane Chester. Mel and Dee were arguing over the *New York Times* crossword puzzle when Mr. Braderman suddenly began to shush them. He waved his hands for silence and turned up the volume on the radio.

"It's official now, folks," the newscaster was saying. "That tropical storm we've been watching has turned into a hurricane and begun its sweep up the eastern seaboard. Small craft—"

Mr. Braderman abruptly switched the station off.

"Da-*ad!*" exclaimed Mel.

We've got to find the local news," her father explained.

"We have to find out if Chester's expected to hit Fire Island."

Mel and Dee fell silent. Timmy looked up from his gooey creation. Mrs. Braderman dropped her needlework in concern.

After several frustrating seconds, Mr. Braderman found a Patchogue station. There was no cause for alarm, the weatherman said. Not yet. It was too soon to tell what Chester would do. He could spin out to sea at any time.

But by later that afternoon, the Davis Park police were striding up and down the wooden walkways, using bullhorns to announce that the island was to be evacuated first thing the next morning.

Hurricane Chester was expected to blow right over Fire Island Monday afternoon. Danger was imminent. Damage was expected to be considerable.

Chapter Ten

"Everybody, start packing," ordered Mr. Braderman. "Right now. You kids start on your rooms."

"Should we bring everything home?" asked Timmy. "I mean, even the stuff we usually leave here?"

"No, we'll never get on the ferry if we try to do that."

"But if we leave things here, they're going to get destroyed."

"I don't think so, honey," said Mrs. Braderman. "We have the boards for the windows, and we'll pack things away carefully. The house has survived other storms."

Mel and Dee went to their room and pulled their suitcases out from under their beds. The cases were dusty and sandy, having been there for over two months. The girls packed quickly, piling belongings on their beds. Then Dee checked the closet and the bureau drawers to make sure everything was empty.

Mel began to worry. Would Justin and his father know what to do to their house? Would Mel really get to say good-bye to Justin? What if Hurricane Chester prevented them from seeing each other?

Mrs. Braderman interrupted her thoughts.

"Throw out anything you don't need anymore," she said, tossing a garbage bag into the room. The bag was followed by a broom. "Then sweep up," she added.

"Boy," said Mel, gloomily. "This is some way to end the summer. All of a sudden today is our last day, instead of tomorrow. And we're spending it getting ready to escape a hurricane." And I may never see Justin again, she thought. It was a tragedy.

It seemed that everything that could possibly be cleaned or cleaned out was given a thorough once-over that afternoon. Mel carted bags of trash to the cans at the end of their walk. She made sure the cans and their lids were chained down and hoped the garbage men would collect the trash before Hurricane Chester arrived.

Mrs. Braderman and Timmy cleaned out the kitchen. They set aside food for dinner and breakfast, then threw away any leftover perishables. The rest of the food— canned goods, spices, tins of flour, boxes of cake mix, and anything else that wouldn't go bad—was packed into boxes and stored in a closet.

Mr. Braderman and Dee struggled with the boards for the windows. They were stored under the house, and hauling them onto the deck was a major job. The boards hadn't been used in several years and were filthy. Dee hosed them down before Mr. Braderman disconnected the hose and put that away, too. "We'll board up the windows last thing before we leave tomorrow," he said.

Shortly before supper, the rain stopped falling. Mel stood on the deck and surveyed the sky and ocean. Both were a silvery gray. The color might have been pretty if Mel hadn't known what it foreshadowed. She saw Lacey on her deck next door.

"Can you come over?" Mel called.

"For a few minutes," Lacey replied. She dashed, barefoot, down her walk and up Mel's. "Can you believe it?" she asked, looking around at the boards for the windows and the hasty packing that was going on in the Bradermans' house.

Mel shook her head.

"You know what I heard?" Lacey whispered. "This one radio station said that if Chester hit hard enough, Fire Island could end up under water."

"You mean—flooded?" asked Mel, shivering.

"No, I mean *gone*. No more island."

"You're kidding!"

"Nope."

"But Lacey, that's horrible!" exclaimed Mel, tears coming to her eyes. "Can you imagine never being able to come back here? Never having another summer—"

"Mel, it's not going to happen."

"But you said—"

"That's the *worst* the storm could do. Come on. Fire Island has been around forever. It's survived plenty of hurricanes. It'll be fine."

"Then why are they evacuating us?"

"Well, would you want to be this near the ocean during a hurricane?"

"No, I guess not."

Mel and Lacey looked at the leaden sky.

"I can't believe the summer's over," Mel said after a moment. "And we got cheated out of our last day."

The Bradermans ate a quick supper. Afterward, Mel couldn't stand it any longer. The rain had not started falling again, so she slipped out of Moonrise and ran to the beach. She just had to have one last visit with Justin, and she knew they might not see each other the next day as they had planned.

When she reached his house, she walked toward it, across the sand. It looked closed up already. Closed up and dark.

Mel's heart began to pound. Had Justin's father decided to leave? Had he packed up Justin and Leila and their things and gone back to the safety of New York? Justin had said he would say good-bye. Still, what was the point if they weren't going to see each other again?

Mel approached the house. She could hear nothing but the crashing of the angry waves behind her. Slowly she climbed the flight of steps until she stood above the dunes. Remembering her dream, she actually checked behind her for chattering teeth, then giggled nervously for being so silly.

She walked to Justin's house and knocked softly on the side door.

Nothing.

She knocked a bit harder, but by then was sure that Justin, his father, and Leila were gone.

Tears smarting at her eyes, she turned away.

She was halfway down the walk when she heard the door open behind her. "Mel?"

It was Justin's voice.

Mel whirled around. "Justin! I thought you were gone! I thought you'd heard about the hurricane, and your house is so dark, and—"

"Hey, it's all right. We were having a candlelight supper. . . . Are you crying?"

"No, of course not."

"Let's go sit on the beach. It won't be very special tonight—no stars or moon—but the ocean sounds nice."

"Okay." Mel hastily wiped her eyes. Then, hand in hand, she and Justin walked back to the beach. The sand was wet from the day's rain, so they sat on an overturned rowboat that belonged to the lifeguards. Mel was surprised that it was still on the beach. By the next morning, she knew, it would be gone—stored away with the other island things, to be brought out again after it had weathered Chester.

"Are you all packed?" Mel asked Justin.

He had made another hand sandwich and was playing absent-mindedly with her fingers. "Yup. It didn't take long. We don't have that much stuff out here."

"Do you know how to board up the house?"

"Oh, we don't have to do that—which is a good thing,

since we *don't* know how. The people who own the house are going to come over early tomorrow to batten down the hatches. It's their responsibility."

Mel nodded. "I wish we weren't leaving tomorrow."

"I know. But Dad found out he gets the equivalent of one day's rent back, since we have to evacuate."

"That's not what I meant," said Mel with a smile. "Even if we had our last day, I wouldn't want to leave. I never do. But it's worse this year. I don't want to leave you."

Justin sighed. "I don't want to leave you either, but . . ."

"I know. Just a summer romance. Why can't we be friends, though? That way, we could both go out with other people—provided I meet guys who are actually interested in—"

"In a hazee?"

"Yeah. And we could see each other, too. As friends."

"It wouldn't work. Would you really want to get together with me, thinking that I've dated other girls? I know it would be hard for me, thinking *you've* been dating."

"I guess."

"It would be one thing if we could just continue our relationship, but we can't. We won't. We live in different towns, my mother's moving to L.A., and Dad and I won't be back here next summer."

"Well, at least let's exchange our addresses and phone numbers. Couldn't I send you a Christmas card?"

"You want a Christmas card correspondence? Like old

friends who're never in touch except to send some dumb message. You know: 'This happy card is sent your way, with love and hope and cheer, to brighten each and every day, throughout the coming year'?"

Mel giggled. "I'm serious. Maybe I'll want to call you after my first day at Bronxville High to tell you whether I've been defaced."

"Well, give me your address and phone number," said Justin finally. "There's no point in giving you mine. With Mom moving, Dad's gotten the urge to move, too. He wants a bigger apartment in the city, and he's been hunting around. He expects to move by the end of September. So I don't know where I'll be. I'll have to send you the address when we get settled. I'll send you Mom's in L.A., too."

Mel sat thoughtfully for several minutes. "Justin," she said, "are you afraid of getting hurt or something? Are you afraid I'll dump you, so you're going to dump me first?"

"I'm not dumping you!" exclaimed Justin.

"Well," said Mel, "I've never been dumped, but this is how I always imagined it would feel."

"Really? You feel that bad?"

"No," admitted Mel. "I guess I don't really feel so bad. I'm just sorry we won't be seeing each other anymore."

"That makes two of us." Justin drew Mel close to him and kissed her softly.

In front of them, the waves poured endlessly over the

sand. Coming and going, thought Mel. The waves were a little like her and Justin. Justin had come into her life and was leaving. Maybe that was the way things were. Coming and going, arriving and leaving, greetings and farewells.

When Mel and Justin drew apart, they stood up, hands clasped for several moments. Then they separated, Justin crossing the sand toward his house, Mel heading down the beach to Moonrise.

They didn't say good-bye.

The next morning passed in a blur. Mrs. Braderman woke the family up early. "Eat," she commanded. "I don't want any leftover food."

They ate hurriedly. Then Mel, Dee, and Timmy began piling suitcases and cartons in the living room while their parents started to board up the windows. It wasn't easy. The rain had started falling again, but by then it was no gentle rain. And by the time Mel, dressed in a long yellow slicker, joined her parents, the rain was lashing down, stinging her face.

"Chester may arrive sooner than they predicted!" Mr. Braderman shouted over the roar of the wind. "Mel, tell Dee and Timmy to load up the wagons. We're almost done here, and I want to leave as soon as possible."

The wagons were loaded in the living room, which was strangely dark and muffled with the windows boarded. Dee covered their belongings with tarps. When everyone was ready, they took a last look at the house, checking things here and there—the burners on the stove, the locks on the windows—then headed for the dock, the rain streaming down their slickers. They paused at the end of the walk to Starfish House.

"Hey, you guys! Hey, Lacey!" Mel shouted. "Are you ready?" The Reeders' house looked just as lonely and alien as the Bradermans'.

"We're coming!" Lacey called, poking her head out the front door. In a moment, the Reeders, slicker-clad and loaded down, emerged from their house. The two families made their way to the ferry dock.

The line for the ferry was the longest Mel had ever seen, since every single person in Davis Park was leaving. But officials assured the people that two ferries were running and that they were going back and forth as fast as they could.

Sure enough, it wasn't long before the Bradermans and the Reeders found themselves near the head of the line. They unpacked their wagons, and Mel and Timmy and Lacey and Jackie ran the wagons back to their houses and stored them under the decks.

A few minutes later, they were boarding the *Kiki*. As Mel reached the top of the little gangplank, she turned for one final look at the frightened, stormy island. Instead she saw Justin. He was near the end of the line, standing with his father and Leila, leaning against a pillar, watching Mel solemnly.

Mel looked back at him. Then she stepped inside the ferry.

Her Fire Island summer was over. Justin Hart would become a memory.

PART II
Bronxville

Chapter One

Melanie Braderman walked slowly up the driveway to her house, a look of surprise on her face. She had survived the first day of her freshman year at Bronxville High.

She did not have a red *F* on her forehead.

Timmy flew across the front yard toward her. "Hey! Where is it?"

"Where's what?"

"Your *F.* I thought for sure—"

"You thought wrong, squirt. Nobody even knew I was a freshman. But wait a few years and *you'll* get an *F.*"

Fear flashed across Timmy's face, then he recovered, stuck his tongue out at Mel, and ran down the sidewalk.

"Where are you going?" Mel called after him.

"Over to Matthew's. Mom knows."

"Okay." Mel picked her way through the branches and

leaves that littered the front yard of the Bradermans' Tudor house. Chester had done his damage there late Monday afternoon. He had moved through several hours after Mel and her family arrived home. He rained and blew and knocked down some power lines so that the electricity went off until the next morning. But he did his worst damage to the east of Bronxville, sweeping directly over Fire Island with all the force gathered from his sea journey up the East Coast.

Fire Island was not, as Lacey had suggested, underwater, but considerable damage had been done. Homes had been destroyed, trees had been uprooted, and the shape of the beach had actually been altered slightly. Then Tuesday morning had dawned unexpectedly bright and clear. Mel thought that if it hadn't been for the littered lawns and the taped-up windows, you wouldn't have suspected it had rained the day before, let alone stormed.

Mrs. Braderman called an acquaintance in Patchogue who owned a house on the island, and asked her to take a look at Moonrise and Starfish when she ferried over to check the damage on her own home. The news, all in all, was not bad. Part of the walkway to Starfish would have to be replaced, Moonrise would need some new roofing, and both houses had lost sections of railing around the decks when heavy tree limbs fell on them, but that was all. The houses were still standing and intact, for the most part. Mel had called Lacey with the good news.

"Hi, Mom! I'm home!" Mel let herself in the front door and stood for a moment in the dark hall. The weather was hot, and Mel appreciated the cool of the quiet house.

"I'm out back, honey," Mrs. Braderman replied. "Come tell me about school."

Mel deposited her notebook on a bench and took her time getting to the back door. She wanted to prepare herself to face the heat again.

She stepped into the heavy, muggy air and found her mother working in one of the flower beds. Mrs. Braderman stood and removed her gardening gloves, peat moss falling from them.

"Well, how's my high-schooler?" she asked with a smile.

"In one piece. And not defaced."

"I guess it helps to have an older sister who knows the ropes."

"Not to mention the boys," Mel added.

"How did Diana fare?"

"Not quite as well. She's coming over as soon as she gets the lipstick off."

"Oh, poor Diana," said Mrs. Braderman.

"She's all right, Mom. You know Diana."

Diana Lyle was Mel's best Bronxville friend. Outgoing, friendly, eager, and sure of herself, she was as different from Lacey Reeder as hot dogs were different from pizza (in Mel's mind). In fact, Diana and Mel were so much alike that they often clashed. Mel was sure that, over the years, they'd been best enemies more often than best friends. But neither one would have known what to do without the other. At the moment, they desperately needed to rehash their first day of high school.

"Are you hungry, honey?" Mrs. Braderman asked Mel.

"There's fruit salad and cheese in the fridge, and granola bars in the cookie jar."

"Oh," moaned Mel, "that's all healthy stuff. Where are the Twinkies? The Yodels? Don't we have any M&M's?"

"Mel, we are back in civilization," her mother reminded her firmly. "I should never have let you eat like that all summer. Your teeth are going to fall out, and your face—"

"Which hasn't broken out yet—"

"—but is bound to any day if you keep eating so many sweets, is going to look like . . . like . . ."

"Like the surface of the moon?"

"*Mel.*"

"You started it, Mom."

"Melanie Braderman—"

"Okay, okay, okay."

"I don't know where you get your junk-food mentality from. Certainly not your father or me," said Mrs. Braderman.

"I knew it. I'm adopted after all," said Mel.

Mrs. Braderman laughed. "All right. Go on inside and eat something—something *healthy*. I've got a summer's worth of neglect to fix in this garden."

Mel returned gratefully to the cool of the house. She carried her notebook into the kitchen with her, then poured herself a glass of orange juice and took a granola bar from the jar. Maybe eating healthy wouldn't be as bad as she'd thought.

Mel leafed through her notebook. Already, she had

homework—several algebra problems and a short essay for English class. She didn't mind. She liked schoolwork.

The doorbell rang. Diana.

Mel ran to answer it.

"Hi," she greeted the girl on the doorstep. She leaned forward, taking a close look at Diana's face.

Diana skinned her short, mouse-brown hair back from her face. "Can you tell?" she asked.

"Not a bit. Well, actually there is a faint red smudge," Mel admitted. "But it's *really* faint. If I weren't looking for a lipstick stain, I'd never notice anything."

"Good," said Diana.

Mel stepped back and Diana entered the hall. After years of friendship with Mel, Diana knew the Bradermans' house as well as her own, yet her first words were, "It's so strange to be in here again."

"I know. It's even strange for *me* to come back to it after two and a half months on Fire Island. For one thing, it feels like a palace. Moonrise House may be wonderful, but it sure isn't big. Speaking of which, did you grow or something over the summer? I don't remember almost looking you in the eye before."

"Two inches," replied Diana proudly. "At this rate, I won't be the shortest kid in our grade anymore, and I'll have to get a new wardrobe. Most of my clothes look like I stole them from dwarfs."

Mel giggled. "Well, come into the kitchen, Stretch. You want a snack?"

"Sure. I figure if I keep eating, I'll keep growing."

"Let's just hope you only grow in one direction. You

wouldn't want to turn into a balloon."

"Never," agreed Diana. "Maybe I'll end up taller than you."

In the kitchen, Mel and Diana sat across from each other at the table, the jar of granola bars within easy reach.

"So," said Mel, "aside from getting tortured, what did you think of the high school?"

"It wasn't bad," Diana replied after a moment. "I like my classes, and most of my teachers seem okay. Except for one, Mr. Bogdanoff. Do you have him?"

Mel shook her head. "What does he teach?"

"Algebra."

"Oh. I have Willis."

"Well, I guess I can survive Bogdanoff, but my brother warned me about him. He said Bogdanoff's tough, and I think he's right. Bogdanoff talked to us for an entire forty-two-minute period and never once cracked a smile. And he uses scare tactics. He kept talking about what would happen if we didn't do such and such."

"I hate teachers who do that!" exclaimed Mel. "I thought we outgrew them in elementary school."

"I guess not. What did *you* think of BHS? More important, what did you think of the boys?" Diana arched her right eyebrow suggestively.

"I think it's too bad that the boys we'll see the most of are the ones in our class. The freshman boys seem to be the same size as they were last year, but the freshman girls seem to have grown. A lot. However, I noticed that the *sophomore* boys seem to be taller, in general."

Diana held an imaginary microphone to her mouth. "Another fascinating anthropological observation from high-schooler Melanie Braderman. Now back to you, Chet."

"Well, anyway," Mel went on, "I wish the guys and the girls would get on the same growth schedule. It would make life much easier."

"Nobody ever said life was easy," Diana replied solemnly.

"Oh, well. I guess it doesn't really matter. I don't plan to see much of the boys at school anyway."

"You don't?" said Diana suspiciously. "Why not?"

Immediately, Mel began to blush.

"Mel!" Diana cried. "You met someone, didn't you?"

Mel nodded, smiling.

"On Fire Island, right? Oh, that's so romantic! I can't stand it! Tell me about him. What's his name?"

"Justin Hart," Mel replied, still blushing.

"Justin Hart," Diana repeated slowly. "Why does that name sound familiar? . . . Is he from around here?"

"No. New York City. He goes to a private school. He's a sophomore."

Diana frowned. "That name is so familiar. . . . Oh, well."

"There must be a million Justins," said Mel. "It's a popular name."

"Right. So tell, tell."

"Well, he's gorgeous. I mean really gorgeous!" Mel couldn't help grinning again. "We met a few weeks ago, and we saw each other for the rest of the summer."

"How are you going to see him now? Are your parents

going to let you go into the city alone?"

Mel paused. She didn't know what to say. On the one hand, she knew that Justin had wanted just a summer romance. On the other hand, he had Mel's phone number and had promised to send her his new numbers and addresses when he could. On the third hand, Mel hadn't heard from him yet; she had thought he might call to find out whether Moonrise was still standing. On the fourth hand, it was only Wednesday—just two days since they'd left the island. On the fifth hand, Justin had wanted just a summer romance. (Mel was back where she started.) Maybe he wasn't going to call at all.

"I don't know," Mel finally told Diana. "I really don't know."

Chapter Two

It was a good thing that Mel decided not to sit around and wait for Justin to call or write. Almost two weeks went by, and she didn't hear from him. She reminded herself about the summer romance. And she reminded herself that she and Justin honestly liked each other. That was a comforting thought when doubts set in. Maybe a clean break *was* the best way to end things. Justin had been right. It would be too difficult to see each other now that school had started.

Besides, Mel thought, there were some cute boys at BHS; there were even some cute boys in the freshman class. P.J. Perkins, for instance. Of course, he wasn't as cute as Justin, but he was nice. At any rate, he was taller than Mel.

Mel finished her homework and flopped on her bed.

She looked around her room. She liked her room, even thought it was very different from Diana's and from her other friends'. Their rooms were modern, furnished in high tech with brightly painted walls and furniture.

Mel's was old-fashioned. Her furniture was from her grandmother's house—heavy and dark and antique. The wallpaper was a pattern of tiny yellow and pink roses between narrow green stripes. On her walls were framed pictures. Mel didn't like posters. She supposed she was old-fashioned, which was why she was sitting around waiting to hear from Justin.

"This is ridiculous," Mel said aloud, and stood up. "I am not going to moon over Justin."

She left her room and walked down the hall, passing Timmy in his room playing with his computer, and Dee in her room, doing her homework. She trotted down the stairs, past her parents in the living room (Mr. Braderman reading, Mrs. Braderman paying the bills) and went into the den to watch television.

Mel, however, was not a big TV watcher and had no idea what was on. She started to channel-hop but was overwhelmed by the cable box and its thirty-six channels.

"Mom?" she called. "Does today's paper have a TV section in it?"

"I don't know, hon. Look for the *TV Guide*. It's in there somewhere, probably buried under the magazines."

"Okay. Thanks." Mel began pawing through the stack of magazines on the table next to her. Her parents subscribed to practically everything in the world: *Newsweek, Ms., Psychology Today, Good Housekeeping,* the *New*

Yorker. At last she found the *TV Guide*. She started to flip through it, then checked the date. Last week's. Mel tossed it aside.

Immediately she snatched it up again. What was that ad she had seen? She opened to the center of the magazine, held it closer, and stared at it. Parading across the two-page advertisement were the actors and actresses who were going to be featured in the new fall shows.

And right in the middle of the crowd was Justin!

At least, Mel thought it was Justin. A curly-haired boy with big eyes smiled at her from the left-hand page.

I'm going crazy, Mel told herself. I'm starting to imagine Justin. That could be any curly-headed, dark-eyed, freckle-faced boy . . . couldn't it? It was so hard to tell.

The top of the ad read, "Watch for the *TV Guide* Fall Preview issue—coming soon." The Fall Preview issue. That was where Mel could find out who the boy in the ad was. Mel made another frantic search for the current *TV Guide*. She found it at last, but it wasn't the Fall Preview issue. It must be next week, she decided.

Mel finally selected a program and turned it on.

"Oh, great," she thought. "Just in time for the commercials." The show faded out, and a man in a blue uniform came on to talk about toilet bowl cleanser. Then a woman fed her family frozen dinners and fed her dog All-Natural, Thirteen-Vitamin, High-Energy Dog Chow. After that, came a newsbreak, and then a commercial for *People* magazine.

Old covers of *People* spun across the screen at a dizzying speed, so fast that Mel could barely identify the faces on them. Then the cover of the most recent issue flashed on and stayed on for just a second longer than the old covers had. Mel tried to identify the face she had seen. It had been that of a young, good-looking boy — dark, curly hair, wide brown eyes, a sprinkling of freckles. It looked an awful lot like . . .

Now I really *am* crazy, Mel thought. If Lacey were here, she'd tell me I was zooey, zany, off my rocker, and in outer space.

I'm seeing things — hallucinating. Justin. Was. Not. On. The. Cover. Of. *People*. Magazine. I'm going Justin-crazy.

Mel reached over and picked up the receiver of the phone that sat next to the magazines. She dialed Diana's number.

"Hello?"

"Hi, it's me. I think I'm going crazy," said Mel.

"Why?"

"Why what? Why am I going crazy?"

"No, why do you *think* you're going crazy?"

"Because I keep seeing Justin everywhere. I'm going Justin-crazy. Every curly-haired, dark-eyed boy looks like him. I thought I saw him in *TV Guide* and on the cover of *People*.

Diana laughed. "You need to get him off your mind, Mel. And you know the best way to do that?"

"No. What?"

"With another boy."

"What other boy?"

"Any other boy. Is there a guy at school you like? Even

an upperclassman? It doesn't matter whether he's within your reach. All you want is a chase."

"What?"

"In fact, the further out of your reach he is, the better, because the harder he is to catch, the better the chase will be."

"Are you saying I need to chase a boy sort of as a hobby? Something to keep my mind occupied?"

"Yes. Exactly. Who do you like?"

"P.J. Perkins."

"Hmm," said Diana slowly. "I don't know. I mean, I don't know how much of a chase he'll provide. He *is* good-looking, and he *is* nice, but since all the freshman girls are looking at the upper-class boys, the freshman boys have more competition than they know what to do with. Still, P.J. was the president of the eighth-grade class. He was sort of a big-man-on-campus last year. Maybe that's held over. Yeah . . . he might be a good one to chase."

"I'm glad I have your approval." Sometimes Diana could be very trying.

When Mel and Diana finally hung up the phone, Mel calmly looked up the Perkins' number in the phone book. Eight Perkinses were listed, but P.J. had his own phone, so that made life easy. Even though it was the first time Mel had ever called a boy, she didn't feel a bit nervous, which only went to show, she thought, that she had, in fact, been made totally loony by Justin Hart.

P.J. picked up the phone after the first ring. "Hello?"

"Hello, P.J.?"

"Yes?"

"This is Melanie Braderman. I sit two rows away from you in—"

"Melanie! Hi!" P.J.'s voice sounded both softer and more excited than usual. He knew who Mel was! What a relief. That made life easier, too.

"Hi," Mel said again. "How are you?" (Oh, no. What a *dumb* thing to say. Justin and Mel had talked so easily. Maybe it was because they'd been face to face.)

"I'm fine. How are you doing?"

"I'm fine . . . too." (Aughh.) "Well, what I was wondering is . . . do you want to go to the movies on Friday?"

"Sure. What's playing?"

"Rocky Thirty-five."

P.J. laughed. "What's really playing? Oh, well. It doesn't matter. We'll find something to go to."

"Okay," said Mel. "See you tomorrow."

"See you."

They hung up. Mel had made her first date with a boy.

Chapter Three

The next day, Wednesday, Mel was in a daze because of what she'd done the night before. She'd called a boy— a popular boy—and asked him to go to the movies with her, and he'd said yes. Just like that.

Diana had nearly killed Mel because no chase had been involved. No chase whatsoever. But Mel pointed out that her mind certainly had been taken off of Justin. Diana had to agree.

After school that day, Mrs. Braderman drove downtown to do some errands, and Mel and Dee went with her. While their mother was in the lingerie shop, the girls browsed through a magazine store. Dee immediately headed for the beauty magazines, while Mel checked out the tabloids (or "rags," as Lacey called them). She looked them over eagerly. "Live Alien Found in Cow's Stomach," she read. "Baffled vet thought cow was pregnant." She glanced at another. "Possessed Car Drives Owner to New Jersey."

Mel smiled. Then she turned away from the tabloids. She knew the real reason she had wanted to go in the store, and it was time to do something about it.

Mel found the shelf with the current issues of the most popular magazines on it, and scanned it for *People*, as well as for the new issue of *TV Guide*, which she hoped would be the Fall Preview issue. She found the *TV Guide* first. Bold red letters on a banner across the front of the magazine assured her that it was, in fact, the Fall Preview. Mel picked it up without bothering to look inside, and continued her search for *People*. She couldn't find it anywhere.

"Can I help you, miss?" someone asked.

Mel turned to find a store clerk at her elbow. "I'm looking for *People* magazine," she said. "The newest one. I was sure it would be here somewhere."

"It is. It's been going like hotcakes, though. Has that new star on the front—what's-his-name. Jason somebody. Pete's bringing another load in from the back. If you'll wait just—Oh, here he is now."

A young boy was struggling toward the front of the store, staggering under a huge stack of bundles of magazines.

"Got a new *People* in there for the little lady?" the store clerk asked the boy.

Pete dropped his load ungracefully at Mel's feet. "Sure,"

he replied. He looked through the bundles, selected one, untied the strings that bound it, pulled out a magazine, and handed it to Mel.

It was backside up. Mel closed her eyes and turned it over.

She opened her eyes.

Justin smiled up at her from the cover.

It really was Justin. No question about it. Mel could do nothing but stare down at his handsome face.

"Everything all right?" she heard Pete ask.

Mel was unable to answer him.

The clerk shook his head and shot a knowing look at Pete. "Crazy teenager," he muttered.

Pete grinned and went to work untying the rest of the bundles.

Still, Mel could not move. She held the *TV Guide* in one hand and *People* in the other and stared down at Justin Hart.

"You want to buy those," the clerk asked, "or just stand there and stare at 'em?"

Mel snapped back to reality. She realized that the clerk was losing patience with her and hoped that Dee hadn't noticed. But Dee was across the store, looking at fashion magazines.

"Buy them," Mel replied. "Thank you." The clerk stepped behind the cash register at the counter, and Mel handed him the magazines and a five-dollar bill. He slipped the magazines into a bag and handed it and the change back to Mel.

She threaded her way through the racks to Dee. "We better go," she told her shakily. "We're supposed to meet Mom in a few minutes."

Dee didn't look up. "Okay," she replied vaguely. "Mel, how do you think I would look if I got my hair permed?"

"Like a poodle." Mel was anxious to go home. She wanted to read her magazines, but she wanted to read them in private, although she wasn't sure why.

Dee returned the copy of *Seventeen* to its place on the rack.

"Are you going to buy anything?" asked Mel.

"I don't know." Dee noticed Mel's bag. "What'd you buy?"

"Oh . . . nothing."

"'Oh . . . nothing' always means something. What is it? *Scientific American*?"

"You wouldn't be interested."

"Probably not. All right, let me just find out if they have the new *People,* and then we'll go."

"They—they don't!" Mel said hurriedly. "I just asked."

"They don't?" Dee looked so disappointed that Mel felt guilty.

"The clerk said they've been selling like hotcakes."

"Oh. *Darn.*"

"What's wrong?" asked Mel.

"Everyone at school's talking about the guy on the cover. They say he's absolutely dreamy. I'm dying to see the article. Oh, well. Somebody'll bring it to school tomorrow."

Mel and Dee left the store, Mel carefully steering Dee in a path that avoided the rack of current magazines. They met their mother at the car.

By then, Mel was frantic to get home, escape to her room, and open the cover of *People*. No, she didn't even want to open the cover—at first. She just wanted to stare down at Justin's gorgeous face . . . and try to figure out what it was doing on the cover of a magazine.

Silently she urged her mother through every red light and stop sign. When Mrs. Braderman finally pulled into their driveway, Mel was out the door before the ignition had been turned off.

"What's Mel's hurry?" she heard her mother ask.

"Don't know," replied Dee. "She was acting funny in the store, though. It's probably just a stage she's going through."

Mel was too panicked over Justin to bother to defend herself. She tore upstairs to her room, closed her door, flung herself on her bed, got up again, locked the door, and returned to her bed.

At last she could read in peace.

She withdrew *People* from the paper bag as if she were handling a rare jewel. Holding her breath, she gazed down at the cover—at Justin's head of dark curls; at the freckles marching from cheekbone to cheekbone, crossing the bridge of his nose; at his gray eyes. Mel knew Justin well enough to see that even though he was smiling broadly, the smile was his shy one. She kept looking at him and noticed a small space between his top front teeth. "Why didn't I see that before?" she wondered.

Mel remembered that the store clerk had referred to Justin as "that new star." However, he had also called him Jason, so maybe he was wrong. Maybe Justin wasn't on the cover because he was a star. Maybe he had done something really important, like developed a radical, new, nonpolluting form of energy. Or maybe he was a self-made millionaire.

Gingerly, Mel opened the magazine to the table of contents. Cover story—page 56. She then opened the magazine, turning directly to page 56, and wondered if that were some sort of sign. She took a deep breath and began to read about Justin Hart.

When she finished, she let the magazine slide off her lap. She leaned against the headboard in a daze. Justin was a star. No, he was more than a star. He was the hot new teen idol. He was going to be what Ricky Nelson had been to young fans in the fifties, or what Michael J. Fox was to fans in the eighties—known by all, enjoyed by most, and adored by most girls.

Mel sighed.

A year or two earlier, Justin had scarcely been known. He'd done some modeling, he'd done some voice-overs, and he'd appeared in several commercials. Mel remembered the commercials mentioned in *People* and tried to place Justin in them, but she couldn't do it.

Then, in the past year, he had made two movies and been cast in the central role of Zack in a new television series. Everything was breaking at once—the movies, the TV show, and lots of articles and attention. (Justin's press agent must be working overtime, Mel decided.) Soon the face of Justin Hart would be as familiar to the American public as the face of the president of the United States.

Mel flipped through *TV Guide,* looking for a description of "It's No Joke," the show Justin would star in. She found it, along with a posed photo of the cast members and a close-up of Justin. The caption under it read: "Meet Justin, the nation's new 'Hart-Throb.'" Mel groaned, then scanned the blurb about the show.

"*'It's No Joke,'*" it read, "*the continuing story of the Brodys, a family facing today's problems with a sense of humor.*" She read on. The rest of the cast included a mother, a father, a grandfather, an older brother, a little brother, and a younger sister.

Mel took a close look at Tania Delaney, the girl who played Zack's sister, Susannah. She seemed to be about Mel's age, but was entirely too pretty. In fact, she was gorgeous.

Suddenly feeling shaky, Mel slapped the *TV Guide* closed and leaped up. She needed to talk to somebody, but not anyone in her family. They wouldn't have answers, just star-struck questions, and questions were not what Mel needed.

As silently as she could, Mel crossed her room and stood at her door. She listened for a moment. Not a sound. She turned the lock, opened the door, and peeped into the hallway. More silence. Mel tiptoed into her parents' room, closed the door, sat down on their bed, and reached for the phone.

She dialed Lacey's number.

Ring . . . ring . . . ring . . . ring. Mel let it ring fifteen times before she gave up.

She returned to her bedroom and closed the door again.

Why, she wondered, had Justin kept the truth from her?

Chapter Four

It was impossible for Mel to keep her secret a secret. By the end of school the next day, it seemed as if the whole world knew about Justin Hart and Melanie Braderman.

Things started in the cafeteria at lunchtime. Mel, brooding, was just settling down at a table with Diana and two other girls, Valerie and Jane, when Dee ran over to them, waving a copy of *People*.

Mel realized what was coming. She wished she were an ostrich so she could bury her head in the sand.

"Mel! Mel!" shouted Dee. "Have you seen this? Have you *seen* this? It's *Justin. Your* Justin! The guy everyone's talking about is *Justin Hart!*"

Mel nodded slowly. "I know." (Why couldn't Dee have confronted her at home?)

"You *know?*" Dee repeated. She pulled up a chair and

107

sat down with Mel and her friends. Mel figured that Dee must be out of her mind with excitement. That was the only way to explain a junior voluntarily sitting at a table with a bunch of freshmen. "You mean all last month you knew about this and kept it quiet?" Dee regarded Mel with a look that was annoyance mingled with surprise and respect.

"What?" asked Diana. "What about Justin Hart... Mel?"

"Yeah... what?" echoed Valerie and Jane.

"Mel met this guy on Fire Island over the summer. They went out for an entire *month*," Dee explained.

"You *did?*" Valerie and Jane's eyes grew as wide as saucers.

Diana's practically dropped out of their sockets. "The guy you told me about is Justin Hart? Oh, wow—your Justin is this Justin!"

Mel slid a fraction of an inch further down in her seat. She nodded miserably.

"And you *knew?*" Dee asked again.

Mel didn't know what to say. She didn't want to lie, but she felt foolish admitting that, in fact, she was as surprised as Dee and her friends were. Her astonishment at Justin was slowly mixing with anger. He had humiliated her.

Suddenly Mel stood up. She had decided that she didn't have to answer any questions. "I don't feel like discussing it," was all she said. Leaving her uneaten lunch behind, she stalked out of the cafeteria.

* * *

Mel did her best to avoid her sister and friends in school that afternoon. She knew she owed Diana and Dee, at least, some sort of explanation, but she couldn't face them. Not yet.

The first thing Mel did when she got home was ask permission to lock herself in her parents' room and phone Lacey, something she should have done the previous afternoon when she tried to call her. She warned her mother that it might be a long call and said that she would pay for it when the bill came. Mrs. Braderman, seeing that Mel was upset, immediately gave her permission and didn't ask any questions.

Mel settled herself on her parents' bed. She checked her watch. There was a good chance that Lacey wasn't back from school yet. She usually took the subway home, and, since Mel had been on the subway herself several times, she was surprised Lacey ever made it home at all, let alone late.

But she dialed the Reeders' number anyway.

Someone picked up after the second ring. "Hello?"

"Hello . . . Lacey?" Mel found it hard to tell Lacey and Jeanmarie apart over the phone.

"Yes . . . Mel?"

"Yeah, it's me. I'm *so* glad you're home. I really didn't think you would be."

"Mel, I *raced* home today. I mean, I took a *taxi* from school just to get home as fast as possible." Lacey's voice sounded breathless and excited.

"You did? Why?" asked Mel. "What's up?"

"What's *up?* Are you kidding? Have you seen *People* magazine?"

"Oh. . . . Yes. That's why I'm—"

"Can you believe it?! Justin was famous, or almost famous, and he never let on . . . did he? Did he tell you?"

"No."

There was a pause.

"Mel?" asked Lacey. "What's wrong? Something's wrong. I can tell."

"Well, I'm *mad,* that's what's wrong. This is so humiliating. I feel like a fool. Everyone is running around waving copies of *People* in my face and being impressed that I went out with Justin Hart, and then I have to admit that *I* didn't know he was a big star—or going to be a big star—either. Why would he keep that from me?"

"You mean," said Lacey after a moment, "you really didn't know about *any* of this?"

"Not a word. If I did, I would have told you. I tell you everything. . . . Why do you think he did this?"

"I don't know. But you know what I think you should do?"

"What?"

"Call him and ask him point blank."

"I can't."

"Sure you can. You're Melanie Braderman. You're not afraid of things like—"

"It's not that," Mel interrupted Lacey. "I don't have his phone numbers or addresses. He didn't give them to me because he said both his parents were moving this month. He said he'd give me the new numbers and addresses later."

"Well," said Lacey practically, "I'm sitting right next to a New York City phone book. I'll just look his parents up for you. We'll find out where they are now."

"Oh, Lacey! What a great idea! Why didn't I think of that?"

"Hold on just a sec." Mel could hear a thunk as Lacey put the receiver down, and then the sound of pages turning. After a moment, Lacey got the phone again. "I hope you know his parents' first names," she said. "There are three and a half columns of Harts."

Mel groaned. "I don't know. I mean, I think Justin mentioned the names, but it'll take me a while to remember them. . . . Lacey, tell me the truth. Why do you think Justin kept all this a secret?"

Lacey sighed. "Well, he's shy. He probably just didn't want to talk about himself too much."

"But it was almost as if he lied to me. He mentioned his work in New York a couple of times, but he never said what it was. I assumed he was, I don't know, a clerk in an office, or a gofer or an assistant somewhere. But he must have been filming instead, probably working on the TV series. You know what *I* think? I think I was convenient. I think I was someone nice to pal around with in a place where he didn't know anybody, but now that he's a star, he can have his pick of starlets. He doesn't need me anymore. Did you see that gorgeous Tania Delaney who plays his sister? She's a hundred times prettier than I am. And she's glamorous—"

"Mel," said Lacey, "stop it. I wish you could hear yourself."

"But think about it," Mel rushed on. "This must be why he didn't give me a phone number. He didn't want me to call him. He doesn't need plain, skinny old Melanie Braderman anymore."

"Mel, *stop,*" Lacey said sharply. "I didn't get to know Justin very well, but from what I saw, he seemed honest and straightforward . . . and just plain *nice*. What I want you to do is get off the phone and think seriously about your relationship with Justin. Try to remember conversations you had, and the things he said to you and how he looked when he said them. After you relive it all, if you still think the whole thing was a farce, *then* you can worry."

Mel took Lacey's advice. When they got off the phone, she went to her own room, stretched out on her bed, crossed her legs, put her hands behind her head, and leaned against the wall. She remembered that the first time she had met Justin, Timmy had injured him. Justin had seemed pleasant but eager to be on his way. He had looked like a loner.

She remembered that *she* had made all the next moves—following Justin and spying on him—and that she had been interested in him—even concerned about him—because he was always by himself.

She remembered that Justin hadn't taken any interest in her until he had been overcome with curiosity about the person spying on his house with binoculars.

What did all that tell her? It told her that Justin wouldn't even have noticed her if *she* hadn't gone after *him*. On the other hand, Mel reminded herself, once Justin had become interested in her, he hadn't (as far as she knew) paid attention to any other girls in Davis Park, even though there were gorgeous, available ones (like Lacey) everywhere you looked. Justin had chosen Mel and stuck with her.

She felt a bit better.

Then, as Lacey had suggested, Mel tried to remember some of the talks she and Justin had had. She recalled reciting the Robert Louis Stevenson poem with him. Then bits of actual conversation came back: Justin saying, "The sun's out and I thought maybe we could take a walk." And "I've only known you for two days, but it feels like a lot longer. . . . I wish it didn't feel so long. . . . Because it's going to be so hard to leave." And other things— talks about freshman year and fights with friends and how it feels to be a "divorced" kid. Would Justin have said those things, divulged those feelings, to someone he didn't really care about? Mel didn't think so.

She felt even better.

She tried to conjure up Justin's face. When she couldn't do it vividly enough, she pulled *People* out from her desk drawer and gazed at him. Slowly she found herself lost in the feelings of their first kiss, lips meeting tenderly, hearts pounding.

With a rush of pleasure and relief, Mel realized that she was still in love with Justin Hart, and that he was in love with her, or at least had been over the summer. She thought she understood why he had wanted just a summer romance, but she didn't know why he had kept his work a secret from her. And she felt she had a right to know.

Mel decided that summer or autumn, phone number or no phone number, she had to see Justin once more. She had to talk to him. The question was—how?

Chapter Five

By dinnertime that evening, Mel felt much better. Which was a good thing, because Timmy had gotten hold of *People* at school and had shown the article about Justin Hart to Mr. and Mrs. Braderman. The whole family then knew Mel's secret, and they were full of questions and speculation.

"What a surprise!" Mrs. Braderman exclaimed. "Did you know about this, Mel?"

Mel tried to be honest without appearing stupid. "Not exactly," she replied.

Dee looked at her sharply.

"I mean," Mel went on, "I knew his father was a big-time producer, and I knew Justin was working this summer, but I didn't exactly know . . . how famous "It's No

Joke" would make him. . . ."

"To think we knew him, had him over for dinner," said Mr. Braderman.

"He seemed very unassuming," added Mel's mother, "even shy."

"Lots of actors and actresses are shy people," Dee commented.

"He was so nice to me!" Timmy said excitedly. "I told everyone in my class how we played volleyball together."

"Are you going to keep seeing him?" asked Dee.

That was the question Mel had been dreading most of all. "I don't know. It's not going to be easy to get together with him. Even if he were a regular person, it wouldn't be easy. His mom's moving to L.A., so he'll be back and forth between California and New York, and I don't get into the city very often. I just don't know what will happen. Besides, tomorrow night I'm going out with a boy from school."

Timmy dropped his fork with a clatter. "You *are?* You mean like on a *date?*"

"Yeah," said Mel. "Like on a date."

"Ohhh," moaned Timmy.

"What's your problem, squirt?"

"You're dating."

"So?"

"That means *two* crazy sisters hogging the bathroom and getting hysterical over their makeup and losing important things right as the doorbell rings."

Mel laughed.

"Who's the lucky boy, sweetheart?" Mr. Braderman asked.

"Yeah, who is he?" echoed Dee with interest.

"P.J. Perkins," replied Mel.

Timmy started laughing and fell sideways out of his chair. "P.J.?" he shrieked as he straightened up. "Like pyjamas?"

"No," Mel answered with great dignity. "P.J. like Paul Jeremy." She turned to her parents. "We're going to the movies. Since P.J. can't drive yet, we're just going to meet at the theater. If one of you drives me there, you can meet him."

"That's fine," said Mrs. Braderman. "How are you getting home? I could pick you up after the show and give P.J. a lift."

"Thanks," replied Mel. "I'll have to ask P.J."

Dee looked as if she had a few more questions for Mel, but she saved them until dinner was over. When the kitchen had been cleaned up and Mel was in her room, seated at her desk ready to start her homework, the door slightly ajar, Dee knocked softly.

"Can I come in?" she called.

"I guess." Mel was getting tired of talking about Justin.

But Dee's questions were about P.J.—and dating. "Aren't you excited, Mel? A real date, with a high school boy!"

"I had several real dates with Justin," Mel pointed out. "It's not like this is my first one."

"But this is different. I mean, it's normal. Fire Island

is fantasy land. This is the real world."

Mel just nodded. She didn't want to say anything about how much she liked Justin because she didn't want any more questions about him.

"So," Dee went on, "what are you going to wear tomorrow?"

"I don't know."

"What are you going to do with your hair?"

"My hair? Nothing."

"Makeup?"

Mel shrugged.

"Mel!" Dee exclaimed in exasperation. "How much thought have you given to this date?"

"Well," Mel replied slowly, "not, for instance, as much thought as I've given to the global problems of terrorism and population control. Probably not even as much thought as I've given to my homework tonight."

Dee made a face. "Mel," she said, "dating is serious business. Don't you want to look nice tomorrow?"

"Don't I look nice now?"

"All right, don't you want to look special tomorrow?"

Mel frowned. She was being difficult, and she knew it. Less than two months earlier, she'd been complaining that she'd never been whistled at, never been asked on a date, wasn't as pretty as Dee. She should have been ecstatic over her date with P.J. and pleased that Dee was giving her such attention. But there was a problem, and Mel was well aware of it. She loved Justin, and she didn't feel the same way about P.J. P.J. was nice (and tall), but

as far as Mel was concerned, that was all there was to
it.

On the other hand, Dee was hanging around, practically
begging to help Mel with her hair and makeup and clothes,
and Justin might very well be—what was her father's
term?—a pie in the sky, something she could never hope
for.

Mel softened. "Dee," she said, "could you help me?
Maybe give me a few more tips on blusher and stuff, and
look through my closet with me? I do want to look nice
tomorrow."

"Special," Dee corrected her.

"Right, special," Mel repeated, grinning.

Mel and P.J. were going to the seven-thirty movie and
had agreed to meet at the theater at seven-fifteen. At
seven, Dee gathered Timmy and Mr. and Mrs. Braderman
in the living room.

"Get ready!" she cried. Then she called up the stairs,
"Okay, Mel, make your entrance!"

Mel walked slowly down the staircase.

"Here she is, folks," Dee continued, "wearing designer
jeans, a baggy pink, very chic sweat shirt borrowed from
her sister, and new shoes, purchased just this afternoon.
Her hair is by Dee (that's me), and so is her makeup.
May I present to you, Melanie Braderman!"

Timmy and Mrs. Braderman clapped enthusiastically,
and Mel's father let out a low whistle.

"Honey, you look absolutely lovely," said her mother.

"Thanks," replied Mel. "I hope P.J. thinks so."

"If he doesn't, then he's a jerk," said Timmy.

"Shall we go?" asked Mrs. Braderman. "You don't want to be late."

"Okay," agreed Mel. "And Dee—thanks for all your help."

Dee smiled. "Any time."

"I promise to bring your sweat shirt back in mint condition."

When Mrs. Braderman pulled up in front of the theater, Mel whispered urgently, "There he is. . . . Oh, he sees us. He's coming over. Just stay in the car, Mom. I'll introduce you to him and then you drive off, okay? Don't get out or anything."

"All right." Mrs. Braderman smiled.

"Promise?"

"Promise. Just remember to find out if he needs a ride home."

In a moment, P.J.'s round face was looking uncertainly into the Braderman's car. Mel rolled the window down. "Hi," she said. "P.J., this is my mom. Mom, this is P.J. Perkins."

"Hi, P.J.," Mrs. Braderman said warmly.

"P.J., do you want a ride home after the show? My mom can drop you off."

"Oh, sure. That would be great."

"What time should I pick you up?" asked Mel's mother.

"How about ten o'clock?"

"Ten o'clock!" cried Mel.

"Yeah. I thought we'd get something to eat after the movie. We could go to Fitzwillie's."

Mel looked at her mother.

"That's fine," said Mrs. Braderman. "I'll see you there. Have fun!"

Slowly, Mel got out of the car. She had almost hoped her mother would say no to Fitzwillie's.

She and P.J. walked to the ticket window, and Mel pulled out a five-dollar bill.

"Oh, no. I'll buy your ticket," said P.J., pushing a ten-dollar bill toward the ticket-taker.

"No, thanks," said Mel quickly. "I'll buy my own." Somehow, it had seemed all right for Justin to treat Mel every now and then, but she didn't feel comfortable with the idea of P.J. treating her.

"What'll it be?" the woman in the ticket booth asked P.J. "One or two?"

"Two," said P.J.

"One," said Mel. "Really. . . . You know, women's lib and all that."

"Okay," said P.J. "One." He turned to Mel. "But *I'll* buy the popcorn."

Mel smiled and gave in. "All right."

She and P.J. found seats in the theater, and P.J. draped his jacket over the seat next to Mel while he went to the lobby for popcorn. The previews were just starting when he returned. He sat down and balanced the popcorn on the armrest between himself and Mel.

Mel ate a handful, then concentrated on the screen. It

went black for a moment, then tiny white letters appeared in the middle and loomed larger and larger. When Mel could read them, she realized they were the title of an upcoming movie: *Holding On*. More tiny letters appeared under the title and slowly blew up.

Mel caught her breath.

The new words read simply: "Starring Justin Hart." And under them: "Coming Soon."

Mel's heart began to pound. She stiffened, staring rigidly at the screen. The black background faded to a scene in a classroom. The camera was behind the students, and only the backs of their heads were visible. Slowly it circled to the front of the room. It zoomed in on one student—Justin Hart.

His face filled the screen, looking gorgeous and serious, just as Mel remembered it.

She wanted to die. She wondered if P.J. could tell that she was on the verge of a nervous breakdown. But P.J. stared placidly ahead.

Later, Mel remembered little of the movie they saw. P.J. had apparently enjoyed it. At any rate, he had laughed all the way through. And when he and Mel went to Fitzwillie's later, he reenacted most of it for her. Mel was grateful. It meant that she didn't have to talk much.

When they left Fitzwillie's at ten o'clock, Mrs. Braderman was waiting. She followed P.J.'s directions to his house. "Mel?" said P.J. as he got out of the car.

"Yes?"

"Do you want to go out again next Friday?"

Mel paused. P.J. was nice. He was considerate. But he wasn't Justin. On the other hand, Justin might as well not exist.

"Sure," Mel replied. "Thanks. See you Monday?"

"See you Monday."

The date was over.

Mel decided that she felt like an old shoe.

Chapter Six

The days passed slowly after Mel's date with P.J. She tried to concentrate on things that wouldn't remind her of Justin, but somehow everything reminded her of him.

The following Wednesday was the debut of "It's No Joke." Mel decided to watch it at Diana's house. The idea of watching it at her own house was not very appealing. She knew that Dee and Timmy and even her parents (who all planned to watch) would talk about Justin as if they had known him intimately—which they hadn't. Furthermore, Diana was going to be the only one at her house that night. Her older brother had left for college and her parents were going to a school board meeting. Watching with Diana would be the next best thing to watching in private.

Mel had long since apologized to Diana for her outburst

in the cafeteria. Ever since, Diana had been especially tactful on the subject of Justin.

"So you *really* liked him?" she had asked Mel during study hall one day.

Mel nodded. *"Really."*

"But what happened? Why haven't you been in touch with him? Did you guys have a fight?"

"No. We just . . . It isn't going to work out, that's all." Mel would not admit the truth to anyone but Lacey.

After a moment, Diana said, "Remember when you first told me about Justin and I said his name sounded familiar?"

"Yeah."

"I finally realized why. It was because I had just read a magazine article about kids in commercials. There was a paragraph on Justin. Did you know that he used to be the My-T Soft Diaper baby?"

Mel giggled. "Really?"

"Yes," said Diana, not pausing to say anything about Mel's not knowing. And then she was off on another subject. Mel was grateful.

On Wednesday, Mel arrived at Diana's a half an hour before "It's No Joke" was to come on. "Oh, good," said Diana. "You can help me make popcorn."

"You need *help?* You've got a popcorn popper."

"Don't be a jerk," said Diana mildly. "We're making Fudgy Popcorn in honor of the occasion. Here, melt these chocolate bars in the double boiler."

Diana's popcorn invention turned out to be delicious.

Mel put a plate of it on the table in the TV room. Then she and Diana settled themselves on the couch. Diana turned the television on with the remote control and switched it to channel 4.

Mel glanced nervously at her. "I feel like I'm about to watch someone audition or take a test."

"I guess it is a test, in a way," said Diana. "I mean, the show's supposed to be a hit and everything, but no one's seen it yet. The people in the audience are the ones who will really decide whether the show is popular."

"Shh!" Mel said suddenly. "Here it is! Here it is!"

The words "It's No Joke" appeared on the screen with lively music playing in the background. Then came a shot of a residential street. It could have been any street in any town in America. The camera rolled down the street past several homes, then slowly zeroed in on one house. After a moment, it zeroed in even closer on an upstairs window. A girl, Tania Delaney, came to the window. Her name flashed tastefully across the bottom of the screen. Gorgeous Tania smiled a gorgeous smile.

Mel stuck her tongue out at her.

The camera moved to the next window, and another character was introduced. Window by window, everyone in Justin's TV family was presented to the viewers.

"But where's Justin?" Mel asked in frustration. "Everyone's been introduced already—even the adults and the dog."

"Wait, wait! There he is!" exclaimed Diana.

The camera had pulled back slightly and the front door of the house opened. Justin stepped out. In large letters appeared the words "And Starring Justin Hart."

"Wow," breathed Diana. *"Starring.* He's the *star* of the show!"

"Yeah," Mel said softly.

Diana glanced at her, about to say something, then changed her mind and turned back to the set.

Mel thought that the plot of the first "It's No Joke" was not really very special. In the story, Susannah Brody, the character played by Tania, wants to start dating boys, and Zack (Justin) suddenly becomes an overprotective big brother and does all sorts of wild things to ward off any possible dates. Nothing new. Mel had seen it all before.

However, Mel thought that the actors and actresses were wonderful, especially Justin. They made a mediocre script into a very funny show. Mel even had to admit that Tania was good.

As the final credits were rolling, Diana turned to Mel and said, "I don't know about you, but I loved that! I plan to be sitting right here on this couch from eight-thirty to nine every Wednesday evening from now until the show is off the air."

"Oh, you know I liked it, too," Mel replied. She and Diana had laughed nonstop during the show. They had laughed so hard that they'd missed some lines and had had to keep turning to each other and saying, "What? What did he say?"

Suddenly Mel began to giggle. "Remember when Susannah's first date, Joel, arrives at the house and Justin meets him at the door in the gorilla suit?"

Diana began to laugh, too. "Yeah, and Joel says, 'What gives?' and Zack goes, 'What do you mean, what gives? It's Wednesday—Gorilla Day. Isn't Wednesday Gorilla Day at your house?'"

"And Joel turns around and runs home!" Mel finished up. Then her smile faded. "Diana, tell me honestly. What did you think of Justin?"

Diana pretended to swoon. "I thought he was . . . Gosh, 'gorgeous' doesn't seem like a good enough word for him. I'll use that just for his looks," she decided. "I think there's a lot more to him than good looks. He seems warm and—and funny, of course—and caring. I feel silly saying that when all I know of him is what I saw on a half-hour TV program."

"No, you're right," said Mel. "He's all those things." What Mel didn't add was that she was more in love with Justin Hart than ever. "The nation's Hart-Throb." That was a pretty accurate description, she thought. Mel made up her mind. She would call Lacey as soon as she had a chance for a private conversation.

Mel got her chance the next evening. While Dee and Timmy were busy with their homework, and Mr. and Mrs. Braderman were having coffee in the living room, she closed herself in her parents' room and dialed the Reeders. Mel had realized that she might be calling Lacey a lot and had decided to stop asking permission each time. She would deal with the phone bill when it arrived and her parents hit the ceiling.

"Lacey," Mel said as soon as Lacey was on the phone,

"did you see 'It's No Joke' last night?"

"Are you kidding?" cried Lacey. "Sure! It was great. It was all anybody could talk about in school today."

Mel hadn't planned to ask it, but the question slipped out of her mouth: "What did the girls say about Justin?"

"Oh, they're all in love with him. They said what a hunk he is and how cute he is. One girl said she was having a Hart attack over him. They're thinking about starting a Justin Hart fan club. They say they'll call it Hart Beat."

"I was afraid of that," said Mel.

"What do you mean?"

"Not only is Justin tempted by that Tania Delaney every day on the set, but now he's got every girl in America falling all over him. Look at my competition. How can I beat that?"

"Mel, are you saying—"

"I'm saying I've decided I'm not giving Justin up without a fight. But what a fight it's going to be—me against millions of girls having Hart attacks."

"But you *are* going to fight back?"

"Well, I decided that at least I want to talk to him one more time. If nothing else, I want to find out why Justin kept all this stuff a secret and why he wouldn't give me his phone number. If he doesn't want to see me anymore, fine. But I have a right to know those things. And it wasn't fair of him to leave our relationship unfinished, especially when he knew I'd find out about him so soon."

"All *right!*" said Lacey. "Good for you. What are you going to do?"

"First, I'm going to try to call him. Even a phone conversation would be all right at this point. Now, I've remembered his parents' first names. Do you have the phone book there?"

"Yup," replied Lacey, "and I'm opening it to *Hart.*"

"Okay," said Mel. She waited several seconds. "Have you got it?"

"Got it. Go ahead."

"His mother's name is Jade."

"Jade?" Lacey repeated in astonishment. "Jade Hart? What a name!"

Mel giggled. "Really. I know."

"Let's see. . . . Gosh, there aren't any Jade Harts listed, but there are fourteen J. Harts. . . . Hey, maybe his mother goes by her maiden name, since she and Justin's father are divorced. Do you know her maiden name?"

"No," replied Mel, discouraged. "Well, let's try his father. His father is Madison Hart."

"Madison Hart . . . Madison," murmured Lacey. "Well, no Madison Harts, but twenty-one M. Harts."

"Just for kicks," said Mel, "see if any Justin Harts are listed."

"No," said Lacey a few seconds later. "No Justins. Hey, do you know where he lives?"

"No. And I'm not going to go calling all those J. Harts and M. Harts asking for him. It would be embarrassing."

"I don't blame you."

Mel thought for a moment. "Lacey?"

"Yeah?"

"What are you doing a week from Saturday?"

"Why?"

"How'd you like a guest? I feel like going into the city and eating at Serendipity and shopping at Bloomingdale's. I could use a change of pace. I'm sure Mom and Dad would give me permission."

"I think it would be great. I'd love to see you."

"Oh, thanks! I'll call you next week to tell you what train I'm taking. Will you meet me at Grand Central?"

"Of course. At the information booth?"

"Sounds good. Talk to you later. 'Bye, Lacey."

"'Bye, Mel."

Chapter Seven

The days between Mel's phone call to Lacey and her trip
to New York seemed endless, even though they were
punctuated by P.J. Perkins. First there was Mel's date
with him on Friday, the day after Mel had phoned Lacey.

They went to the movies again, and afterward met some
of P.J.'s friends and ate French fries at Hugh's House of
Hamburgers. P.J. and his friends talked about the Bronxville High football team for over an hour. Mel barely said
a word. She decided that P.J. was tired of her. But he
called her at home three times the next week, and twice
they ate lunch together in the cafeteria. Then she didn't
know what to think.

When they were alone, their conversations were, Mel
decided, more interesting than talking about football with
P.J.'s friends, but far less interesting than the dullest con-

versation Mel had ever had with Justin. On a conversation scale of one to ten, P.J. rated a five, and Justin rated an eighty-two.

On Thursday evening during the third phone call, Mel began to wish that P.J. would stop calling her. It was at that moment he said, "Mel? I've kind of been wondering. Would you like to—to be a couple? You know, not go out with anyone except each other?"

Mel felt her mouth drop open. "Be a couple?" she squeaked. No. No, she did not want that. She also didn't want to hurt P.J.'s feelings. "Gosh, P.J.," she managed to say. "I'm—that's really flattering. But that's . . . a big step. I don't know if I'm ready to, like, commit myself to someone. Can I think it over?"

"Sure," he replied.

Mel knew she was going to have to tell him no eventually. She wondered if she was making a big mistake. She was going to turn down P.J., a sure thing, for a shot at Justin, a pie in the sky.

Mel had a fairly easy time convincing her parents to let her take the train into New York to visit Lacey. The Bradermans trusted Lacey and knew that Mel and Lacey needed to see each other from time to time. Furthermore, ever since the beginning of September, they had seemed to trust Mel more than usual. Mel couldn't tell if it was because she had entered high school and become a responsible ninth-grader or if it was because she had actually had a relationship with a major television star. Whatever the reason, she was glad to be allowed to visit Lacey.

The girls planned their meeting carefully.

"The train gets in at eleven-oh-three," Mel told Lacey at least eight times.

"Okay. I'll be waiting at the information booth in the main room."

"What if I can't find you? Remember that time I went out the wrong door and wound up in the subway system?"

"It won't happen again. I promise. Just follow the crowd. They'll all be heading for that central room. Then once you get to the room—"

"It's the one with the paintings on the ceiling, right?" asked Mel.

"Right. Once you get there, *ignore* the crowd and just look for the information booth. I promise I'll be there."

"At eleven-oh-three."

"At eleven-oh-three."

Whenever Mel went to New York, much as she enjoyed the trip, she felt as if all her insecurities poured forth, while Lacey's sophistication took over.

Mel's trip into the city that Saturday was uneventful. The train was crowded, but Mel still managed to end up with a window seat. She had brought two magazines along for the ride—*Star Gazer* and *What's Hot*. Each carried a feature story on Justin Hart, America's Hart-Throb. Mel read them with a combination of eagerness and dread. She didn't learn anything about Justin she didn't already know, except that reliable sources were already carrying rumors of a possible romance between Justin and the gorgeous Tania Delaney.

By the time the train arrived in New York, Mel had a lump in her throat. But it disappeared when she saw Lacey waiting for her at the information booth.

"Lacey!" Mel called.

Lacey looked around, searching the crowd for Mel's face. "Hi, Mel!" she cried a moment later.

When Mel managed to squeeze her way through the crowd to Lacey, the girls threw their arms around each other.

"Gosh, I've missed you," Mel exclaimed. "It feels like months since we've seen each other, instead of just a few weeks."

"Oh, I've missed you, too!"

Mel stuffed her magazines into her bag as they walked along. For some reason she didn't want to lose the articles on Justin. In fact, over the weeks she'd saved everything she'd read about him, including the little blurbs from *TV Guide,* describing what was going to happen on each episode of "It's No Joke."

"So," said Lacey as they hurried through the crowds in Grand Central, "what do you want to do first? I made a reservation for lunch at Serendipity for one o'clock, so we have almost two hours before it's time to eat."

"Bloomingdale's," Mel replied promptly. "Let's go to Bloomingdale's. But let's walk there. Can we? Is it close enough?"

"About fifteen blocks," replied Lacey.

"Oh, no problem. We'll walk, then. Okay? Let's go up Lexington."

"Your wish is my command," said Lacey.

The girls walked slowly up Lexington Avenue. Mel, who was almost always in a hurry in Bronxville, was rarely in a hurry in New York City. She had long ago decided that it was because there was nothing interesting to see in Bronxville, while everything in New York was interesting.

"Even the pigeons are interesting," Mel said to Lacey, who was well aware of Mel's thoughts about the city. "See? Look at those two pigeons on that windowsill. They're kissing."

Lacey looked in the direction Mel was pointing. Sure enough, two pigeons were kissing on a windowsill. Lacey sighed and shook her head. "I never notice things like that."

"That's because you've grown up here. You're jaded."

Lacey smiled. "Country mouse, city mouse," she said.

Mel and Lacey kept passing newsstands as they walked toward Bloomingdale's. Mel liked to look in them, since there were no newsstands in Bronxville—at least none like the ones on Lexington Avenue, which seemed to sell everything from jewelry to coffee and doughnuts—but she tried hard not to look too carefully. Almost every stand also carried a variety of newspapers and magazines on the entertainment business, and Mel saw Justin's face on most of them. She felt that that was highly unfair, since she was in New York supposedly to forget about Justin and her boy problems in the first place. On the other hand, Mel felt drawn to the newsstands. She couldn't keep her mind off Justin anyway—magazines or no magazines.

In Bloomingdale's, Mel and Lacey scoured the jewelry department. They pretended that they had five thousand dollars apiece, just to spend on jewelry, and for almost a half an hour they gazed into glass cases, picking out the diamond earrings and gold necklaces they would buy.

When they left the jewelry department, they looked at shoes and clothes and makeup.

"Almost time for lunch," said Lacey as they were paying for jars of liquid blusher.

"Really?" replied Mel. "Wow, the time went so fast." She leaned over to Lacey and whispered, "Where are the rest rooms? Do I have time to go to them before lunch?"

"Sure, if you hurry," said Lacey. "I'll show you where they are. I'm going to look at stockings while I wait for you."

"All right," said Mel uncertainly as Lacey pointed her in the direction of the ladies' lounge. But almost immediately, Mel was glad she was on her own, because she found two Justin things. The first was a whole row of telephones with brand-new phone directories in some of the booths. Maybe, thought Mel, Lacey's phone book was old and out of date. She stopped in a booth, opened one of the new phone books, and checked all the names in Justin's family that Lacey had looked up for her.

Nothing.

The other thing she found was a copy of *Variety*. It was the most recent issue, and it was lying abandoned on a couch in the lounge. Mel, attracted by Justin's name on the front page, took several minutes to flip through it. When she found the article on Justin, she tore it out and stuffed it in her bag. She didn't bother to read it, since she didn't want to hold Lacey up.

Even so, after she left the rest room, she found that she couldn't pass by the phones again without stopping to call information. She asked for all the names connected with Justin that she could think of. To some, the operator said, "We have no listing under that name." To the others, he said, "I'm sorry, that number is unlisted."

"But couldn't you just give it to *me?*" asked Mel, knowing full well that he couldn't.

"I'm afraid I can't do that."

"Please? I'm a good friend of Justin Hart's. Really."

"You and several thousand other kids," said the operator.

"What?"

*"Every*body wants Justin Hart's number."

"Oh," said Mel.

"Sorry. Have a nice day. Thank you for calling AT&T."

"Any time." Mel hung up, dejected, and ran to find Lacey.

"Where *were* you?" asked Lacey. "I was about to come looking for you. We're late. It's one-oh-five already."

"I'm sorry," said Mel, feeling sorrier than was necessary. "There was a long line for the bathroom. Let's go."

The girls hustled out of Bloomingdale's and ran to Serendipity, which was only a couple of blocks away. The restaurant was very crowded, but their reservation seemed to be good, even though they were late. A waiter showed them to a table on the second floor next to a huge fireplace. It was quieter and less busy there, and Mel felt as if she could relax a little.

As soon as they sat down and the waiter had left, Lacey began to giggle. "What?" asked Mel.

"I should have gone to the rest room with you at Bloomie's. Now *I* have to go. I'll be right back."

Mel watched Lacey thread her way to the stairs. When she was out of sight, Mel dove for her bag and pawed through it for the article from *Variety*. She scanned it eagerly, her eyes opening wider and wider.

Then she read it again.

Mel could not believe what she was reading.

Chapter Eight

By the time Lacey returned to the table, Mel had made an effort to calm down. She had read the article a third time, put it away, sipped some water, and scanned the giant menu the waiter had left on the table.

She was sure she looked normal.

"Do you know what you're going to have?" Lacey asked her.

"I think so," replied Mel. "How about you?"

"Oh, I don't even need to look at the menu. I always get the same thing here. Jeanmarie says that's really boring, but I *like* it."

The waiter appeared, took their orders, and disappeared with the menus.

Mel sat back in her chair and tried to act as casual as

possible. "So," she said. "Do you have any idea where Lincoln Center is?"

"Of course," replied Lacey. "Why?"

"Oh, just wondering."

Lacey frowned. "Is there something you want to see there? Lincoln Center is mostly for ballet and opera and stuff. I didn't know you liked that kind of thing."

"I don't. Not at all," replied Mel honestly. ". . . How long do you think it would take to get there?"

"It depends on how we go. By bus, about twenty minutes if we're lucky."

"Is it open today?"

Lacey sighed. "Yes, it's open. But what do you want to do there? I thought we could go to Rockefeller Center this afternoon and see the TV studios or something."

Mel hesitated. "Could we do both?"

"*What* is going on at Lincoln Center? I don't know if we can do both until I know what you want to see over there."

"Justin," Mel finally whispered, looking into her lap.

"What?"

"Justin." She raised her head. "Justin and the cast of 'It's No Joke' will be there. So will a lot of other TV people. It's for some benefit."

Lacey narrowed her eyes. "Mel, did you know about this all along? Is this the real reason you wanted to come to New York today?"

"No, I swear," Mel said fervently. "I just found out about it. There was this copy of *Variety* in the ladies' room at Bloomingdale's and I just happened to flip through it and find the article about the benefit. It says it's at Lincoln Center and it's going on all this afternoon. . . . Lacey, please—you were the one who said I should confront Justin and ask him point blank about our relationship and what happened. Well, here's my chance. *Please?* You'd like to see all those TV stars, too, wouldn't you? It would be really exciting."

"Well . . ." said Lacey.

"The entire cast will be there—Tania Delaney and all the others. *And,*" Mel added, "the cast of two soap operas."

Lacey jerked her head up. "Two soaps?! Which ones? Which ones?"

"'Days of Drudgery, Days of Despair'—"

"Mel, you *know* that's not what it's called."

"Well, you know which one I mean. And 'Hearts and Hope.'"

"'Hearts and Hope'? You're kidding! Oh, I can't believe it!"

After that, the meal at Serendipity couldn't go fast enough. All Lacey could talk about were the stars of "Hearts and Hope." And all Mel could think about was Justin. Neither girl tasted her food, and both skipped dessert, which ordinarily was the best part of a Serendipity meal. As soon as they had paid the bill, they dashed onto Sixtieth Street, and Lacey hailed a cab.

"A cab!" exclaimed Mel. "*A cab?*"

"It'll be much faster than the bus," said Lacey. "Look, it's two-thirty already. We don't want to miss anything."

"Or anyone."

"Lincoln Center," Lacey told the driver, "and please hurry."

Ten minutes later, the cab driver, having hurried so much that Mel had been sure they wouldn't get out of the taxi alive, pulled up in front of a crowd of people.

"Are you sure this is Lincoln Center?" Mel asked Lacey. "It looks sort of like the inside of Grand Central Station."

Lacey grinned. "It's Lincoln Center, all right."

Mel and Lacey stepped out of the cab and looked around. Lincoln Center, a group of modern theaters and buildings in a handsome courtyard, appeared to have been turned into a fairgrounds. A bright red banner proclaimed the charity to which all proceeds would be donated—Help for the Homeless. Vendors were everywhere, selling balloons, hats, toys, and candy. Food stalls sold hot dogs, ice cream, pretzels, and even egg rolls.

"This is nice," Mel said, "but where are the stars?"

At that moment, they heard screams and shrieks from a group of people near the entrance to a building.

Mel and Lacey looked at each other. "Let's go!" cried Mel. They ran to the crowd and wriggled through until they were near the front.

"I still can't see anything!" Mel exclaimed. "Can you, Lacey?"

Lacey stood on tiptoe. She craned her neck back and forth. "I think someone in the doorway is signing autographs. I can't see. . . ."

Mel put her hands on Lacey's shoulders and jumped up and down. "It's a man," she said breathlessly after the second jump, "but I don't recognize him."

The crowd opened up a bit and the girls moved forward. Suddenly Lacey gasped.

"What?" cried Mel. "Is it Justin?"

"No, it's *Gregory Standiford!*"

"Who's Gregory Standiford?"

"Oh, he's . . . he's dreamy. He's Rosalind's wealthy brother on 'Hearts and Hope.'"

"Oh," said Mel, disappointed. "Can you see anyone from 'It's No Joke'?"

"Nope," replied Lacey. "I think these are all people from 'Hearts and'—Aughh! There's Roger Russeling! Oh, Mel, I've just *got* to get his autograph." Lacey began rummaging through her purse, looking for paper.

Mel, feeling very small and sorry for herself, was distracted by more shrieking from another crowd of people at another entrance to the building. "Lacey, I'm going to go look for Justin. Why don't we split up for a while? Let's meet in a half an hour at that fountain over there."

"Okay," agreed Lacey. "I'll see you at three-fifteen. Good luck!"

"Thanks." Mel, not quite as hopeful as she had been when she'd first read the article in *Variety,* approached the other crowd and started squeezing her way through. When she was as near the front as she could get, she caught a glimpse of shiny golden hair and then of perfectly arched eyebrows and wide blue-green eyes.

Tania Delaney.

Mel drew in her breath—for two reasons. First, because Tania was even more beautiful in person than in photographs or on TV, and second, because Mel was suddenly sure that where Tania was, Justin wouldn't be far behind.

An amazing number of questions began forming in Mel's mind: How do I stand a chance against someone as gorgeous as gorgeous Tania? Is there any truth to those rumors about Justin and gorgeous Tania? Do I look nice enough to be seeing Justin again? What will Justin do when he sees me? What will I do if he ignores me? Where *is* Justin, anyway?

The only question Mel could answer was the last one. As she stood in the crowd, her mind a dazed muddle, the door opened a second time, and—

There was Justin.

Once again, Mel drew in her breath. Justin looked the way she remembered him from their first meeting on the beach. His dark curls were blowing in the breeze, his summer freckles still stretched from cheekbone to cheekbone, and his wide eyes looked . . . That was where Mel noticed a difference. She realized that she couldn't call his eyes limpid anymore. They looked eager and excited, but underneath the eagerness and excitement was a wariness that had not been there before. She knew in a flash that Justin did not entirely enjoy being surrounded by adoring fans, no matter what his smile seemed to say.

Nevertheless, Mel reached into her purse for a pen and a piece of paper. She found a ballpoint pen but had to make do with an old napkin for paper.

Slowly she worked her way toward Justin and Tania. She had almost despaired of ever reaching Justin when the door opened a third time, and out stepped Peter Mans-ford-Johnson, who played the oldest brother on "It's No Joke." More shrieks arose from the crowd, a number of fans surged toward Peter, and Mel found herself standing in front of Justin Hart.

She held out her napkin and pen. "Hi, Justin," she managed to say.

Justin glanced up and opened his eyes only slightly wider than usual. A hint of pink appeared on his cheeks. Then he ducked his head, scrawled something on Mel's napkin, and handed it and her pen back. Immediately another fan shoved a pad of paper under Justin's nose.

"Please write, 'To Sarah, All my love, Zack Brody,'" she said.

"Zack! Zack!" cried another girl.

Justin was already nearly lost from Mel's sight. Mel edged out of the crowd. Only when she had a bit of breathing space did she dare to look at her napkin.

On it was written: "I love you. 555-2173."

Mel's heart soared. Justin had given her his phone number!

Chapter Nine

Lacey was the only person Mel told about Justin. Given the excitement that had arisen over Mel's summer fling with Justin Hart, she didn't want anyone to know of the possibility that their relationship might redevelop. If it worked out, Mel wanted it to be private, at least for a while. If it didn't work out, Mel wanted it to fail in private.

But Lacey could keep a secret, and Mel had to show *some*body what was written on her napkin.

"I can't be*lieve* it!" Lacey shrieked, nearly falling into the fountain when Mel held the napkin up for her.

"What do you think it means?" Mel asked cautiously.

"It means call him, you idiot! Why else would he give you his phone number?"

"But why hasn't *he* called *me* all this time? He has my

number. What if I hadn't shown up today? Then what? I don't get it."

"Mel, you're thinking too hard. Don't ask yourself so many questions. He gave you his phone number. So call him."

But things didn't seem that simple to Mel.

She spent the train ride back to Bronxville coming up with more and more questions: Why does Justin want me to call him? Why now? Why would he give his phone number to plain old me when gorgeous Tania was standing practically at his elbow? Does he *really* want me to call, or is he just being nice?

Mel decided that Lacey was right. She was overthinking and overworrying the entire matter. By the time she stepped off the train, she had made up her mind. She would call Justin that night. She wasn't sure when he'd be home, but nine o'clock was probably a safe bet. How she was going to wait until nine was another question in itself, since Mel was not a patient person.

However, there was nothing to do *but* wait. Mel showed off her Bloomingdale's purchases to Dee and her mother.

She did some homework.

She played chess with Timmy.

She wrote an extremely sad poem.

Somehow, she managed to keep the napkin a secret.

At nine o'clock, she closed herself into the den, pulled out the napkin, and dialed Justin Hart's phone number.

A lightly accented woman's voice (Leila's?) answered the phone. "Hello, Hart residence."

Mel breathed a sigh of relief. It really was Justin's

number! "Hello, is Justin there, please?"

"No, I'm sorry, he's not. But he's expected home soon. May I give him a message?"

Mel hesitated. (She almost hung up the phone.) Then she said in her most adult voice, "Please tell him that Melanie Braderman called." Melanie gave the woman her phone number.

"Certainly. I'll give him the message."

"Thanks," replied Mel. "'Bye."

"Good-bye."

As soon as she hung up the phone, Mel began to panic. What if somebody else (Dee, in particular) got on the phone and wouldn't get off? How long would Justin keep trying to reach Mel? (Why, oh, *why* didn't her parents have Call Waiting?) What if Justin called back and somebody else answered the phone? What if they recognized his voice? Or worse, what if they *didn't* recognize it and said, "Hold on a minute, P.J. I'll get her."? What if—

Ring, ring.

Mel jumped out of her skin. Then she snatched up the receiver, telling herself it was probably P.J. She tried to prepare for a long discussion of football.

"Hello?" she said.

"Hello . . . is this Mel?"

Mel's heart began to pound. Her knees turned to water. "Yes . . ." She couldn't even bring herself to speak Justin's name.

"Mel, this is Justin."

"I—I know."

"How are you?"

"Fine. . . . How are you?"

"Fine . . . and nervous."

Mel giggled. "I'm nervous, too."

A long, awful pause followed.

"Well," said Justin, "you're probably wondering why I never got in touch with you."

"That, and a few other tiny little things."

"Mel, I'm really sorry," said Justin. "I don't know what else to say."

Mel's heart slowed and her knees regained some control over themselves. "You could say why you never told me about Zack, 'It's No Joke,' *Holding On, People* magazine, *TV Gu*—"

"Okay," Justin cut in. He paused. "Okay." He didn't sound angry, just resigned and embarrassed. "Mel," he said after a moment, "I don't know if you'll believe this, but I really do love you."

"You have some funny way of showing it," she said.

"Just let me finish, Mel. This isn't easy."

"For me either."

"I know, I know. Let me say what I have to say, though."

Mel kept her mouth shut.

"This summer," he began, "one thing I liked about you was that you liked me just because I was me."

"Liked?" Mel couldn't help interrupting. "Why are you using the past tense?"

"*Mel*. Because I'm talking about last summer, *okay?*"

"Okay. Sorry. Go ahead."

"All right. See, I wasn't famous when we first met, but even so, you honestly liked me. That was really important, because . . . this sounds horrible, but I know, for a *fact,* that a lot of people who claim to be friends with my father are not his friends at all. They're people who want things from him—parts in movies, money, invitations to fancy parties, introductions to famous people. And a lot of actors and actresses that I know—well, they don't have friends at all. They just have fans."

Mel was trying to follow what Justin was saying. "What do you mean, they have fans, not friends, Justin?" she asked after a moment.

"I mean, they're . . . Do you remember right after I signed your napkin today, another girl wanted my autograph?"

"Yes."

"Well, she wanted it signed from *Zack,*" said Justin. "She liked my character, not me. And I'm not my character. I *play* Zack Brody for several hours each day when we're shooting 'It's No Joke.' But I *am* Justin Hart. In fact, I'm Justin Herbert Hart."

"Justin *Herbert* Hart?" Mel couldn't help giggling. Then she stopped abruptly. "Okay," she said, "I understand how important a real friend was—is—to you—"

"And you *were* a real friend," said Justin. "I have to admit that at first I thought you might have been one of the few people who recognized me from the commercials I'd done, especially when I found you spying on our house and everything, but I realized pretty fast that that wasn't true at all. You didn't know my name, and you were more interested in Robert Louis Stevenson than in who my father is."

"But Justin," said Mel, "now for the big question. Why didn't you tell me about the TV show and the movies? When I found out about them—and obviously you knew that would happen—I felt like a real jerk. It was so humiliating. Dee was going around telling everyone that you and I had dated over the summer, and meanwhile I didn't know a thing about your career. It made me look awfully silly, or it would have if I'd *admitted* that I didn't know anything."

"I didn't tell you," said Justin slowly, "because I thought it would change our friendship. I liked . . . I loved you so much that I just couldn't bear the thought of our friendship having anything to do with *what* I am instead of *who* I am."

Justin paused and took a deep breath. "Plus . . ." he went on, sounding hideously guilty.

"Why do I have the feeling I'm not going to like whatever it is you're going to say?"

"I don't know," answered Justin, "but you're right, you're not. Plus . . . I didn't want to hurt you."

"What?"

"I knew I was going to be spending a lot of time with Tania Delaney and other girls. I'd work with them, or I'd be asked to take them places—to benefits and award ceremonies and stuff—and I kind of wanted to play the field. You know, see who else is out there. But I didn't want us to worry about that while we were together over the summer. So I figured if you didn't know about my career, then . . ."

"*Is* there anything to worry about?" asked Mel, remembering the rumors of a relationship between Justin and Tania that she'd read about in the magazines.

"No . . . not now."

"So you have gone out with her?"

"Yes. And with several other girls, too. With Meredith Fitzhugh—she guest-starred on the show once—and with—"

"Justin, please. I do not want a list of the girls you dated."

"Sorry."

"Why didn't you just tell me this is what you wanted to do?" Mel asked crossly. She was hurt, and having a hard time covering it up.

"I tried to," Justin replied gently. "I meant it when I said we should be free—both of us—to date other people."

Mel sighed. It was true. He had tried to tell her. And in fact she had gone out with P.J. But for Mel, P.J. was just someone to hang around with since she didn't have Justin, while it sounded as if Justin had shoved her aside because he really *wanted* to date Tania and Meredith and who knows who else.

"So," said Mel after a moment, "you never intended to call me?"

"I don't know," replied Justin. "Not for a long time, I guess."

"And all that stuff about your parents moving—was that a lie?"

"No, it was all true. Mom's already moved, and Dad's found a new apartment. We move in three weeks."

"Well, anyway," Mel went on, "why did you give me your phone number today?"

"Because as soon as I saw you, I knew how stupid I'd been. All I had to do was *look* at you, and I realized how much you mean to me. I knew you didn't care a bit about Zack Brody or the show. You'd come to Lincoln Center just to see me, right?"

"Right. . . . Well, I had a few questions for you, too, of course."

"Yeah. I figured you might be just a little bit mad, so I decided to give you the choice of whether to call me. But Mel, I haven't told you the most important thing yet."

"What's that?" asked Mel, already dreading it.

"That I didn't like any of the girls I went out with."

"Not one?"

"Well, a couple of them were okay, but none of them was *you*. I mean, I didn't feel the same way about them that I do about you."

"Really?"

"Really. Believe me, where Tania's concerned, what you see is what you get. She's false eyelashes and expensive clothes, and guess what's underneath?"

"What?" asked Mel.

"Nothing."

"So you really don't like her? Or the others? I keep looking at the pictures of Tania and feeling so plain and ordinary."

"Mel," Justin said seriously, "anyone who tails me on the beach and lies in the sand dunes spying on me with binoculars because I'm Justin Hart, not Zack Brody, is not ordinary, and is much more my type—and means much more to me—than a million Tanias or Merediths. And now I have a question for you. . . . Would you come into the city some Saturday and spend the day with me?"

"Oh, Justin, you know I would. Just name the day," replied Melanie.

So he did.

Chapter Ten

Because of Justin's hectic schedule, Mel couldn't see him for three weeks. But that was all right—sort of. Mel hated waiting, but she knew she wouldn't have gotten permission to go into the city again any sooner.

Meanwhile, she had things to do. There were school and school activities and Diana.

And there was P.J.

The evening after Mel spoke to Justin, she called P.J. at home.

"Hi," she said nervously when he answered the phone.

"Hi, Mel!" P.J. replied eagerly.

"Listen, I've been thinking about what you asked me, and I'm ready to give you an answer. But you're not going to like it."

156

"Oh . . ."

"P.J., I'm *really* flattered that you wanted to be a couple. It means a lot to me."

"But you're saying no."

"That's right. But only because I simply don't think I'm ready to go out with just one guy. I'm too young for that. We don't want to end up like some old married couple, do we?"

P.J. laughed. "I guess not."

"But I hope we can still be friends and still go out sometimes," Mel went on. "I heard a rumor that *Rocky Thirty-six* is coming to town."

P.J. began to laugh.

By the time Mel hung up the phone, she'd made a movie date (a *"just-friends"* movie date) with P.J., and had told him she was going to bring Diana along. Diana had grown another half an inch and was feeling glamorous. Mel had vague plans for fixing Diana up with P.J.

After what seemed like a year of waiting, the day arrived when Mel was to meet Justin in New York. She had told her parents what she was up to. Dee, Timmy, Diana, and anyone else who cared, thought Mel was visiting Lacey again. Mel couldn't lie to her parents, though, and she knew they would keep her secret.

"Do you understand why I don't want anyone to know about Justin?" Mel had asked Mrs. Braderman in private.

"I think so, sweetheart. And I want you to know how proud your father and I are. Most people would want the whole world to know they were dating someone famous.

You must care about Justin very much to take your relationship so seriously."

"I do, Mom," Mel replied. "We care about each other." She gave her mother a hug.

The next morning, Mel took the train into New York City. She was as nervous as a cat—and not over little things like finding the information booth at Grand Central. She simply had no idea what the day would hold and how she would feel being with Justin again.

When the train stopped at the terminal, Mel got off and followed the crowd into the big room with the painted ceiling. "Wait for me at the information booth," Justin had told her. "But look carefully or you'll never recognize me."

"Why? Do you plan to be in disguise?"

"Yes," he had replied.

"Oh. . . . Maybe we ought to work out a code. Like you say, 'The blue poodle barks at midnight,' so I'll know it's you."

Justin laughed. "You'll know it's me. I'll be wearing sunglasses and a really ugly hat."

Sure enough, Justin was wearing mirrored glasses (Mel hated not seeing his eyes) and an incredibly ugly hat. "Do you have to wear those things all day?" she asked him.

"I do unless you want sixty or seventy other people along with us."

"Wear them," Mel said immediately.

Justin took both of her hands in his, and for a moment,

they stood, linked, simply enjoying being together, joined together. Then Justin leaned over and kissed Mel softly on the cheek.

"I've missed you so much," Mel told him as he drew away.

"I've missed you, too. I don't know how I could have wanted us to be apart."

Mel felt tears spring to her eyes.

Around her, people were hurrying and jostling, calling to one another, cursing the train schedule, and asking harried questions at the information booth. But she and Justin noticed none of it.

"Come on, let's get out of here," said Justin, grabbing her arm.

Mel, hastily wiping her eyes, ran through the crowd with him and outside. Justin hailed the first cab he saw. "Fifth Avenue and Central Park South, please," he told the cabbie.

"Where are we going?" asked Mel.

"You'll see," Justin answered. "It's outdoors where I won't be recognized—I hope. If we went to a restaurant or a movie theater, I'd have to take off my glasses, and then it would all be over in a second."

"You're kidding," said Mel. "It's that bad already?"

"It's pretty bad," he answered, glancing at the cabbie, who was glancing at *him* in the rear-view mirror. Then Justin shook his head at Mel, and they stopped talking.

Several minutes later, the taxi drew to a halt at a busy intersection. Justin shoved some bills through the little tray in the window that separated the driver from his passengers, and he and Mel scrambled out.

Justin took Mel's hand again, and they dashed across Fifth Avenue, passed by a strange piece of modern sculpture, and turned between some hedges. "Do you know where we are now?" asked Justin.

"Central Park?" Mel guessed.

"Right. And we're going to spend the whole day here. You won't believe the things we can do. There're the carousel and the boat pond and the zoo and places to eat."

"Oh, fun!" exclaimed Mel. "What do you want to do first?"

"Well, the zoo's right here. Let's walk around the zoo first."

"So Mel and Justin, hand in hand, looked at the zebras and tigers and llamas and some funny animals called capybaras. They saw a green parrot named Lorita who could say her own name, and they paid a dime each to wander through the children's petting zoo. They walked under the Delacorte Clock, which played a song when it struck the hour and sent its band of statue animals revolving merrily around the top.

Then they walked through the park. They saw a mime and two musicians, a troupe of Russian folk dancers, and a young man performing feats on his fancy roller skates.

When they were hungry, they bought hot dogs and sodas from a vendor and ate them on a bench near a playground. Afterward, they strolled to the sailboat pond, where Justin bought them ice-cream cones. They sat on a bench away from the crowds and licked their cones in silence.

"Justin," Mel said finally, "am I going to see you again?"

Justin glanced at Mel, then turned back to his cone. "Yes," he replied firmly. "But it isn't going to be easy. I really am going to be back and forth between L.A. and New York, and I have almost no spare time."

"I know," said Mel. "But?"

"But how could I ever have said I wanted just a summer romance? We can't do that, you and I."

"If we can't see each other, there's always the phone," Mel pointed out.

"Yeah. We'll just have to make the best of our time. You know, we might not see each other more than once a month. The question is, can we make it work? Is our relationship worth it?"

"Yes," said Mel. "*I* think it is."

"So do I," said Justin.

"I'll tell you something," Mel went on. "When I thought I'd lost you for good, I started going out with this guy at school. P.J. Perkins. He was okay, but I didn't feel anything for him. On the other hand, Justin, I'm only fourteen, and you're only fifteen, so we have a lot of dating years ahead of us. We're *bound* to meet other people we really do like. But I don't think that's a reason for us not go out now. Think what we'd be missing."

"You're right," agreed Justin.

"Boy," exclaimed Mel.

"What?"

"My friend Diana is always saying that life isn't easy. And she's right. School isn't easy, families aren't easy, and *this*"—she extended her arms to indicate her and Justin and their predicament—"really isn't going to be easy. What am I going to do about school dances? You probably won't be able to come to Bronxville, and P.J. might ask me to go with him. What are you going to do about benefits and publicity stuff when you're supposed to have a date along? And what about us? Do we keep our relationship a secret?"

Justin merely shook his head. The problems seemed overwhelming. "All I know," he said at last, "is that we want this to work. Let's cross those bridges when we come to them."

"But let's not burn them behind us."

"Or count our chickens before they hatch."

"Or cry over spilled milk," added Mel, giggling.

When they stopped laughing, Justin went on, "So we'll see each other when we can. Speaking of which—last night I just happened to mention to my father how much I liked the house we rented on Fire Island, and he said, 'Oh, really? Would you like to go back?' and I said, 'Definitely,' and he said, 'Well, I'll look into it, then.'"

"Oh, that's wonderful!" cried Mel. "Just think. Another Fire Island summer together."

"Maybe."

"Maybe."

Mel and Justin tossed their napkins and the remainders of their cones into a nearby trash can. Justin began fumbling in his pockets. At last he withdrew a small package, which he hid behind his back.

"What's that?" asked Mel.

"It's for you." Justin handed it to her. It was a plastic baggie full of sand.

Mel looked at Justin questioningly.

"It's from Fire Island," Justin told her. "To remind you of when we met."

Mel grinned at him. They kissed gently. And then they rose and walked through the park, their fingers laced together.